I0748069

Mob's Seduction

Alyson Root

J&M Books

Human Authored™, Reg #: 4003837, https://authorsguild.org/human

For permission requests, write to a.rootauthor@alysonroot.com

Published by J&M Books

Lytchett House, 13 Freeland Park, Wareham Road, Poole, Dorset, BH16 6FA

Print ISBN: 978-1-917785-03-7

Ebook ISBN: 978-1-917785-18-1

Cover Design By:

Cath Grace @cathgracedesigns

Developmental Edit By:

Tara Sullivan, The Write Gal Co.

www.thewritegal.com

Line & Copy Edit By:

Linda Slate

Proofreading By:

Crystal Lee Wren, COLProof

&

Morgan Bonito

For all the Bookworms in the world.

Mob's Seduction is written in British English.

1

Bonnie

WOOD'S WRITING EMPORIUM, OR simply, "The Emporium", as ninety percent of Twyford, Winchester refers to it, is still dark as I approach. So much for Janice opening up this morning. The woman is as trustworthy as a Nigerian prince wanting to send me twenty million quid via email.

How I wish Clive would hire someone with an ounce of competency. But noooo, old muggins here has to put up with a woman who's older than sliced bread and couldn't care less about running a bookshop—just because Clive nobbled her niece twenty years ago and is still paying for it. Actually, I'm the one paying the price, considering I have to pick up Janice's slack.

Hey-ho, just another wonderful day for me. At least I get to unbox a few new releases today and then read them this evening. That's enough to get me through the working day.

My phone chirps with a notification from my best friend. It's just a string of emojis I decipher in seconds because that's our language now. Ironic, really, how I work in a place that encapsulates and celebrates the English language, yet I opt for a book, teapot, and film emojis to communicate. I'm an embarrassment to the books I so love.

The gist of the message is: Kelley will come round tonight for an evening of reading, tea, and a film that will only serve as background noise. We are rockstars. Some may say we're losers, but whatever. I'd rather carve my eyeballs out with a spoon than go clubbing or raving. Are those still things people do? Hmm, thoughts like that might be why my other best friend, Pete, calls me old, even though I'm mid-thirties.

Speaking of Pete, he has also messaged me with an old granny emoji. Rude. He knows Kelley and I intend to get our literary fiction on tonight and is unsurprisingly disgusted. He may like to gyrate next to sweaty people while hopped up on sugary alcopops, but that's not me; never has been, never will be.

You may wonder why we are friends. That's easy. Pete is a loveable arse who saved me time and time again

2

from school bullies. Really, our friendship shouldn't work because we are very different, yet it does. He likes Kelley too. Occasionally, we all hang out, but mainly I see them separately.

I send him a Face with Tongue Emoji in reply before pocketing my phone. There are only ten minutes left until the shop is supposed to be open. Nothing major would happen if I were a few seconds late. It's not like we have customers lining up outside, but I know for a fact we will have a few regular shoppers turning up to grab the new stock soon.

I unlock and go through the morning routine at double-time. As predicted, there are three regulars peering through the window as I approach to turn the sign that currently reads *Closed* to *Open*.

"Is the new Wallace Skipton book in?" Audrey asks the second the door opens.

"Waiting in the back for me to unbox," I reply, smiling.

Audrey is probably my favourite customer. She's completely batty about books. We've spent many a morning conversing about the latest murder mystery or "romantic panty dropper," as she likes to call them.

In the distance, I see Janice wombling up the street like she's not got a care in the world. I can't even say anything because she'll make up some crap about me being ageist or something, which is laughable. I guarantee I act older than her. She just pulls that particular card when she wants to get out of being responsible for something other than putting the kettle on.

Grumbling to myself, I turn and greet the other two shoppers. Melody and Jasmine are two young art students who are part of the local sapphic book club. I always let them know when something interesting comes in and, of course, we discuss it at length.

God, I love my job.

"Morning," Janice calls. She's as fake as her hair colour.

"Janice, you were scheduled to open up this morning."

"Really? Well, bless my soul, I must have got jumbled up."

My arse she did. I smile sweetly. "Never mind. You can close."

"Oh, but..."

"I have a doctor appointment," I lie. "You don't mind, do you?"

Considering we have an audience, Janice smiles with thin lips, her eyes narrowing. "No, Bon Bon, no problem at all."

I grit my teeth because I detest it when she calls me Bon Bon. Do I look like a fucking hard toffee? No. Janice is just the worst.

Doing a quick breathing exercise, I push Janice and her bullshit to one side. I have boxes of books to unload. We have two new thrillers, one romantic comedy, and one sapphic mafia. I'll leave Janice to do the thrillers. My sights are set on the rom-com and mafia books. I love both genres, as does Kelley, which is why we pre-ordered a copy of each book.

"Bonnie, is that it?" I hear Kelley squeal. I laugh because I should have known she wouldn't be able to wait until this evening to get her hands on the new mafia book.

"Yes, it is, and I cannot believe you didn't even last a couple of hours."

Kelley smiles brightly, her massive curls surrounding her bespectacled face. I've never met someone with such wild hair. It's also the blackest black I've ever seen. I'm pretty sure it actually absorbs light. I was just flipping through a new art book about the mafia-level artist feud over the rights to use the blackest black, but honestly, I still think Kel's hair could give Anish Kapoor a run for his money.

"Momma needs to touch those fresh pages," she says seriously. I roll my eyes before handing over her copy. Of course, the first thing she does is bring the thing up to her nose and take a big whiff. "Oh, yeah!"

"It's like book crack," I joke.

"Butt crack?" Audrey enquires as she rounds the corner. Her arms are already five books deep.

"Book. Book crack," I repeat. "You know, when you get a fresh one and have to smell it?"

"Oh, yeah, totally," she answers. "There is nothing better."

Straight away, I imagine what Pete's reaction would be to this conversation. It makes me laugh.

"Anyway," Audrey continues, "Janice just left. Told me to tell you she suddenly felt squiffy."

My arms drop to my side. She's got some bloody nerve. I look at the giant clock above the cash register. Janice has literally been in the store for less than twenty minutes.

"Whoa, Bonnie, your face is like a really unnatural red."

"I need to make a call," I seethe. Clive is in for an ear-bashing.

"I'll watch the register," Kelley comments, already moving towards the vintage till.

It takes seven minutes of arguing and me threatening to quit before Clive finally gives me the go-ahead to hire a new store assistant. Janice can suck eggs. I'm the one who runs this store on the daily. Clive knows he would be up shit creek if I left—not that I would. I was totally bluffing. I love the Emporium and hope one day, when Clive retires, he'll make me a partner so I can continue the store's legacy.

Feeling my blood pressure drop slightly, I stride with purpose to the cashier's desk where Kelley is finalising Audrey's sale.

"Everything okay, sweetie?" Audrey asks when I stop by her side.

"Perfect. Did you get everything you wanted?"

"Oh, and more. Kelley pointed me in the direction of a new fantasy series I can't wait to get stuck in."

We say our goodbyes and then I twirl in place and face Kelley. "Do you want a job here?"

Kelley's eyes grow wide. "Are you serious?"

"As Clive's stamp collection."

"He finally gave in, huh?" She laughs.

"I told him I would walk out. So yes, he crumbled."

"Then, yes. I mean, let's be fair, I work harder than Janice in this place, anyway."

"That's what I said to Clive when I told him I wanted you on board."

"Well then, it looks like you have a new store assistant." We high five, naturally.

Kelley is an artist. Specifically, she draws comic books, and she's brilliant at it. With it being a freelance job, she tends to be in the bookshop a lot, so this is a perfect setup. Janice will work a few shifts because I couldn't get the old bat fired; I'm not horrible. But at least I now have a chance to really make this place into something. Kelley shares my vision and love of books. We are a winning team. I can feel it!

We didn't last until the close of day before both Kelley and I cracked open Selma Peterson's *Mob's Seduction.* The title needed work, in my opinion, but the story is as gripping as I thought it would be. Plus, it's all about the sapphics, which ticks my box.

"She can't marry her," Kelley gasps.

"She will. It's the only way to save her brother," I respond.

"But the MacLeans are awful."

"Obviously, but Riley doesn't have a choice."

"What about Todd?"

"He's a secondary character. Riley will marry Leah to secure her brother's safety, and then she'll become the consort to Leah and take over the family business!"

"I couldn't do it," Kelley says, shaking her head. "I mean, sure, mafia queens are hot! But to marry one? No, I don't think so."

"Not even to save your brother?"

"I haven't got a brother."

"Hypothetically, you wouldn't marry a hot mafia boss to secure your family's safety?"

Kelley puts down the book and tilts her head. She's doing some deep thinking, which leaves me a few minutes to collect the receipts and put them in the till.

"No," she suddenly says. "I mean, what would my family be doing anywhere near a bunch of mobsters? It'd be their own fault. Why should I give up my freedom?"

"Cold," I laugh, "but you'd still fall in love with the mob queen. That's the whole point of it!"

She shakes her head. "I just don't believe it. In books, yeah, obviously, that's why it's fiction. In reality? No way."

The doorbell jingles, catching my attention because we are ten minutes from closing. Who in their right mind thinks ten minutes is long enough to browse a bookstore? Crazy people, that's who.

Kelley is still waffling on about how inconceivable marrying a mobster to save a family member and then falling in love would be. My attention is on the three humongous blokes who have just stepped inside.

Without taking my eyes off them, I bat Kelley until she shuts up. She goes to ask me what's wrong but then clearly spots the men, who are now splitting up, each taking a different aisle. Why are they still wearing sunglasses? They're indoors!

Placing my book under the till, I straighten and smile. I'm intimidated by the sheer size of them, but I'll try not to show it. Kelley is not doing such a stellar job either as she steps behind me to hide.

"May I help you?" I call to them.

Silence.

The door jingles again. Tearing my eyes away from the men, I look towards the entrance. I really hope it's a police officer.

It's not.

A woman, clad in all black, with platinum-blonde hair slicked back into the tightest bun I have ever seen, stands staring at Kelley and me. The term "deafening silence" comes to mind. It's as though the world outside of the shop has been muted, and the only thing registering is the thick atmosphere these people have created.

"C-can I help?" I ask again, my voice thankfully holding steady—sort of.

The blonde slowly drags her sunglasses off her face. I'm met with stunning eyes; one blue and one green. Jesus, she's like a baddie in one of the thousands of books I've read.

"Bonnie Moorside?" Her voice is rich and deep. Her accent is Italian, I think.

Straightening my back, I pull myself up to all of my five feet and four inches. "That's me," I answer, and then berate myself. Why did I just willingly identify myself to a stranger who looks like she could break my neck with a flick of her wrist?

Her eyes squint ever so slightly, and her gaze roams the top half of my body. I'm sure she'd do a full sweep if the cash desk weren't in the way.

"I've been looking for you."

2

Allegra

I sit in the back of the Land Rover as it cruises along the motorway, listening to Toni and Mia talk. Like me, they are wondering why we have been sent on this mission. We had a full schedule of appointments set for today, all of which are now cancelled. We never cancel, so I understand their curiosity. It matches my own, although I doubt *their* curiosity has turned to burning anger, like mine.

If it weren't for the fact I am devoted to Don Ferrante, I may have lost my cool by now. I cannot abide being kept in the dark, but murdering everyone I know is a little premature, even though my ire calls for it. Until I know exactly what I'm dealing with, I need to keep my temper under control.

For the past six years, I have led the Ferrante family. I might not be blood-related, but Don Ferrante has always treated me as a daughter. He personally told me I would become Donna Malgeri once he was ready to officially retire.

Unlike many other families, he never batted an eye over the fact he hadn't sired an heir. Don Ferrante took me under his wing after my parents were killed by a rival family, and taught me everything I needed to know for my future standing, which was crystal clear until today. He hasn't said anything, but I can feel something is off. My future as head of the Ferrante family is in jeopardy.

I've never seen the Don look so worried as he did when he called me into his home office in the early hours of this morning. His health hasn't been the best of late, but I honestly thought I may end up calling an ambulance when I saw how ashen his complexion was.

His only directive was to travel to the middle-of-nowhere England and find Bonnie Moorside. I tried to get more out of him, but it was useless. He clammed up, which instantly raised my hackles. Don Ferrante has always been an open book with me. I know all his secrets, including the one about how he can no longer effectively run the business, hence the reason I have taken up the mantle in the shadows. To the rest of the family, Don Ferrante is still the powerful leader they all know and trust. But I know better.

But back to the task at hand: finding out who the hell this Bonnie Moorside is and why Don Ferrante wants me to find her? I'm not worried about convincing the girl. I'll throw her in the trunk of the car if push comes to shove. I'm eager to know what the hell is going on, and that means she has to come with me.

"Al, we're here," Toni calls, pulling me from my ruminations. I didn't even realise we'd come off the motorway. I hate being distracted—it's dangerous.

The Land Rover in front of us pulls to a stop outside a bookshop: Wood's Writing Emporium. Interesting name, I suppose.

I get my head back in the game. "Toni, take Mica and Hanz to check it out. Remove any customers if necessary."

"Yes, boss."

"Mia, keep the car running."

"No problem, Al."

Taking my time, I open the car door and step out, always keeping my eyes on my surroundings. There is no threat here, but doing it comes as second nature to me now. The bookshop is quite large, considering the size of the town. We stick out like a sore thumb. Three blacked-out Land Rovers with occupants all dressed in black. We definitely don't blend, but that's fine, I don't intend to be here for long.

My guys have had a few moments to scope out the shop. Time for me to meet this Bonnie woman. The doorbell jingles lightly as I shove it open. It takes me just a second to get a visual of the shop's layout. There is a second exit to the left of the cashier's desk. I presume one of the two wide-eyed women currently staring at Toni and the others, is Bonnie Moorside.

The taller of the two shifts her eyes to me. She's...short. Five-four at most. Her hair is deep brown and swept into a low ponytail. Her clothes are...well, wool. She's clad head-to-toe in wool. I don't need to see below the counter to know that. The woman screams "bookworm cat lady". I'd bet my place as head of the Ferrante family she's wearing a woollen skirt with tights.

"Can I help you?" she stammers. Her nerves are plain to see. Good, I want her on the back foot. Sliding my sunglasses off, I take a few more seconds to stare. Cat-lady aesthetic aside, she's a good-looking woman.

"Bonnie Moorside?" I ask. My eyes roam her chest because, despite the wool, I can see she is well endowed.

"That's me," she answers.

"I've been looking for you." She swallows deeply but keeps her composure. It's impressive. I know how intimidated she must be.

"W-what can I do for you?"

I'd like to smile at her effort. Her friend, on the other hand, looks like she's about to piss herself. "You need to close the shop, pack a bag, and come with me."

There is a beat of silence before she scoffs, "Not likely. Now, if you're not here to buy a book, I need you to leave."

She has guts. Licking my lips slowly, I continue my penetrating stare. Her eyes drop to the tip of my tongue as it travels the length of my bottom lip.

"It wasn't a request," I finally say.

Looking at Toni, I give a curt nod. He walks to the door and locks it, turning the *Open* sign to *Closed* and flicking the deadlock. Stalking forward, I take my time. I want her sweating.

"We're going to leave now," I say in a low, smooth tone, "go to your home where you can pack some clothes, and then you *will* come with me."

"Now, hang on a minute," she argues.

Her efforts are noted. Most grown men who have spent time in prison don't make me ask twice.

"If I have to repeat myself, I will take you by the hair and drag you to the boot of my car," I say calmly.

Her eyes grow even larger with fear. The friend who has been cowering behind Ms Moorside lets out a whimper. I want to laugh. This is turning out to be quite entertaining.

She turns her head slightly and looks over her shoulder, then returns her deep brown eyes to me. "Let Kelley go home, and I'll do as you say."

I place my sunglasses on the countertop. My focus is now on Kelley. "Hmm, how can I be sure Kelley won't call the police?"

"I-I won't, I swear it." She's practically vibrating with anxiety.

Crooking my finger, I beckon her forward. She takes a small step forward. "No. You won't. Because the second you pick up the phone, Kelley, Bonnie is dead." Their collective gasps make me grin. "Is that clear?" She doesn't answer, just nods. "Off you go, then."

I can see the indecision in her eyes. She wants nothing more than to run far, far away, but she also doesn't want to leave her friend. Ms Moorside pleads with her eyes for Kelley to go.

"Unless you want to come along," I say, withdrawing the Glock 20 that's been resting in the waistband holster attached to my trousers.

It makes a satisfying thud as I place it on the counter. The size is intimidating, which is the intent. There's no point wielding a pea shooter. My Glock is weighty, just like the threat I pose when holding it. I want people to be afraid. I want to see the fear in their eyes as I rest my finger close to the trigger.

"In fact, I think that's a much better solution," I finish, revelling in their anxiety.

It wasn't in my plan, but then again, I enjoy a bit of spontaneity. I'll have no qualms dispatching either of them when the time comes.

The two women sit silently in the car. According to her instructions, Ms Moorside's apartment is only a few minutes away. I hope she is correct because I am ready to leave. I want to be back at the house before midnight.

I smile internally when I catch a glimpse of Ms Moorside's wool skirt from the corner of my eye. I'm always right about these things.

Mia pulls over once again. "We're here," she says.

Turning my head to Ms Moorside, who is next to me, I smile. "You have ten minutes. Toni will accompany you. I'll stay here with Kelley and get acquainted."

She wants to argue, but doesn't. Smart woman.

Ten minutes and not a second later, Toni escorts Ms Moorside out of her place and back towards the car. I didn't speak with Kelley. Her crying became too irritating, so I had her moved to the lead car. Now I have time alone with Ms Moorside to find out who the hell she is to Don Ferrante.

"Where's Kelley?" Ms Moorside practically screeches.

"In that car," I say, pointing to the other Land Rover. "Now get in!"

I'm over this. I want to return to work—the work that keeps the family at the top of the food chain. My days of doing this sort of menial shit should be long gone. I feel my anger rising again.

Toni throws her suitcase in the boot and then we're finally on our way home—well, the house we use in the UK.

Home is in Sicily, where I long to be. We are safer, not to mention stronger, when we are there.

It takes longer than I expected for her to finally speak. "Who *are* you?"

"It doesn't matter. I've been sent to collect you."

I want to tell her exactly who I am, to judge her response, but it's better to play it cool for now.

Another few minutes pass before she suddenly starts laughing. She slaps her legs with her hands. "Oh my God, of course," she cackles. "I can't believe I fell for it!"

I have absolutely no clue what is happening, so I stay silent and wait.

Her chocolate eyes turn to me. She playfully punches my arm. "Pete outdid himself this time," she continues, tears of laughter welling up in her eyes. "Where the hell did he find you lot? It was the drama club, right? Of course. Wow, I know he thinks I need some excitement in my life, but this is a bit much."

"I—"

"Kudos for going the mafia route, though. Quite inspired. Although I didn't realise he paid so much attention to the books I read."

"Ms Moorside—"

"God, you are really good as a baddie. Are you a professional actress?"

"Who the fuck is Pete?" I say, my patience waning.

She snorts, "Good one. But you can drop the act. Tell him I'll try to go out more. I won't even take my Kindle."

Grinding my teeth, I breathe out through my nose in an effort to calm myself. "I assure you this is no act."

"Sure," she grins, rolling her eyes.

And then my patience snaps like an overextended rubber band. "Mia, pull over."

She does as I say, instantly. Toni signals the other cars. I haven't got the time nor the inclination to get her to listen to me, so I might as well alleviate some stress and prove a point at the same time. And nothing helps me relax like shedding blood.

We are alone on a country road, which is ideal. I slip out of the car and hold the door open for her to follow. She does, with a twinkle of humour still in her eyes. I signal for Kelley to be let out of the car.

The second Kelley is out and looking my way, I whip the Glock from my trousers and shoot her in the shoulder. It's only a flesh wound, but it makes the point. Ms Moorside is no longer laughing.

She screams, which I expected.

"I am no actor," I say in a level tone, "and the situation you find yourself in is no joke. Have I made that clear?"

I click my fingers to summon Mia, who picks the now shaking Ms Moorside up off the ground. Toni collects Kelley, who has passed out. The bullet was a through-and-through, so she'll only need stitches.

I slide back into my seat and watch as Ms Moorside recoils from me. Don Ferrante only told me to collect the woman. He didn't specify what state she had to be in. Anyway, it's not like *she's* the one with a hole in her body. The Don and Ms Moorside should be grateful. If I let my true feelings out, there would be a lot more carnage.

3

Bonnie

SHE SHOT KELLEY! WITH a gun—a real gun! She just whipped the gargantuan thing out and fired; no hesitation, no remorse.

Oh my God, what the hell is happening? I was so sure this was Pete's hilarious way of getting back at me for always staying in with a good book, but...she shot Kelley! And there was so much blood!

I'm ninety percent positive... No, let's make that ninety-five percent positive, I'm going to have a heart attack. A deep, pounding thrum fills my ears, each beat rattling through my skull and I swear the room is tilting. I might just black out. No pins and needles, though. That's a good sign, I think. I once read about the symptoms of a heart attack. Maybe I'm just suffering a mild one.

Stop rambling and get a grip!

There has got to be a mistake—a huge mistake! The crazy lady has the wrong Bonnie Moorside. I'm a bookstore manager, for crying out loud. What could I have possibly done to have gained the attention of... God, I don't even know who they are! Psychopaths, for sure. Did I mishandle a book order or something?

My brain is conjuring a million things to scream, but my mouth remains clamped shut. I can feel my body convulse with terrified shakes. I'm going into shock, I think.

"Take a breath, Ms Moorside," the crazy killer lady says.

Like *her* voice is the one that will soothe me right now!

I don't fucking think so!

Escape. I need to escape, but if I do, what about Kelley? She might already be dead. The pressure of crazy lady's hand on my arm pulls me from blacking out. Instead, I yank my entire body as far away as possible, which is only centimetres considering I've been plastered to the other side of the car since the driver hauled me off the ground. Fuck, I think I might vomit.

"Mia, pull over again, will you? She's looking a little green."

Is she chuckling at me?

The car comes to a rather abrupt stop. I hear the locks release and instinctively I push myself out the door. My breakfast and lunch make a reappearance. With hands on my knees, I take a few deep breaths. I should run...just start running and hope I find someone to help Kelley.

The tired sigh of the batshit crazy blonde filters through my buzzing ears, "If you run, she dies. It's simple."

Did I voice my plans out loud?

"I—" More vomiting.

"You're not exactly subtle, Ms Moorside."

"Well, forgive me for not wanting to ride along with a homicidal maniac," I spit back. And then I literally spit. Ugh, I need water and a mint.

"Homicidal," she chuckles. "Kelley will be fine. A flesh wound at most. I just needed to make a point."

"And you couldn't think of any other way that didn't involve *shooting* someone to get that point across?"

What am I doing arguing back? This lunatic could finish me off whenever she feels like it.

"Not one that got the point across so quickly," she smiles.

I open my mouth to launch a retort, but I have nothing. My brain is going into sleep mode and I have no idea what to do or say.

"The sooner you get in the car, the sooner I can deliver you and you won't have to see me again."

"What about Kelley? You can't leave her like that."

An eye roll? Really?

"She's already received medical attention. All my men are trained to cope with wounds."

Once I am sure that my bout of sickness is over, I take a second to look at the car pulled up just in front of this one. It's Kelley's car.

"I want to see her!" I demand.

The scary blonde slips out of the car and advances toward me. I gulp—like cartoon-style gulp. I've pushed her too far and now she's going to shoot me too. Pete was right: I haven't had a life. I've spent all my time either selling books, or with my nose in one. I may have travelled to distant lands and galaxies via the printed word, but in reality, I've never left my hometown. How bloody sad is that? And now, I'm going to die at the hands of...

Hang on a minute. She's not reaching for the gun that's wedged near her backside. I watch her come to a stop right in front of me. Craning my head to look up, I whimper as her eyes bore into me once more. When she knows my attention is solely on her, she dips forward. If I didn't know any better, I'd say she was going to kiss me.

But I *do* know better, and I'm more likely to have my throat ripped out by her teeth than any smooching—not that I *want* her to smooch me. Oh, Jesus, I've gone delirious.

Her breath tickles the side of my face as her lips reach my ear, "Please don't make me hurt you, Bonnie," she rasps. "You have such a lovely face." Her head pulls back slightly so I can see her eyes in my peripheral vision. This woman is utterly terrifying. "In the car. Be a good girl."

"I'm not a girl," I growl, before stomping back to the car.

She laughs quietly at my outburst. I'm crossing all my fingers and toes I've contracted a fever or something similar, that would give me an alternative to what is going on right now. Fevered delusion sounds good. I knew I ate too much cheese last night. This could be a really intense dream. Gouda does that to me.

I'm still cataloguing which fromage I snuffled down last night when Blondie slides gracefully back inside the car after I do. She gives a nod to the driver, who says something into a hidden microphone near her cuff before pulling the vehicle back onto the road. Plucking the last vestiges of courage, which are recklessly swimming around my nervous system, I clear my throat. "Who are you?"

"I told you it doesn't matter."

"And *I* beg to differ. You must realise you have the wrong person. Do I look like someone who cavorts with thugs?"

"Thugs?" she laughs. "Come now, Ms Moorside, we both know I'm no thug."

"Government agent?" The question comes out as a hopeful squeak.

"Please, don't insult me," she tuts.

"Okay, just give me your name, then. I can't keep referring to you as 'Crazy Blonde Lady'."

She turns in my direction. "Is that what you've been calling me?"

"Um..."

"I've been called worse. And, it's Allegra."

"Right, Allegra. So, who are you taking me to see?"

My new plan is to keep her talking; maybe get her to relax so I can make a move. If I could get her gun, I could hold her hostage in exchange for Kelley.

Even as I think about it, I know it is a monumentally stupid idea, but what other choice do I have?

My plan held up for all of ten seconds. Allegra is a super spy or something. She can read me in seconds. I know, because as I peppered her with questions, she held up her hand, which stopped me talking and said, "Even if you get my gun, have you ever used one? And saying you manage to work it out before I disarm you, are you ready to take on my men?"

I sat there with my mouth gaping, unable to find an answer, so I just closed my mouth and turned my head away.

I still have my head pressed against the glass of the car window. We've been driving for hours and I need to pee, but I don't want to speak to Allegra again. I want this total nightmare to be over. I've been wracking my brain to figure out who wants to see me so badly, and I'm still at a loss.

I am literally *the* most boring person on the planet; an only child to two wonderful dads. I never had any trouble at school or university. I never hung out with the wrong people, and I pay my taxes and bills on time.

The car slows. The sun fell a while ago, so looking for a clue as to where I am is useless. Allegra doesn't move as her driver steps out of the vehicle. I do my best to listen to what she is saying to the other driver—the one from Kelley's car. There's some nodding and more talking into their cuffs.

The one Allegra called 'Mia' breaks away and heads to Allegra's door. "All clear. We're ready to move."

"Thank you, Mia," she responds and then turns to me. "Do you get seasick?"

I silently shake my head. She's taking me out to sea? I haven't got a passport, so I hope the boat stays in British waters. A burst of laughter echoes around the car and I realise, this time, I *did* say it out loud. Dammit.

"Out," Allegra barks after she's finished mocking me.

Scrambling out of the car, the sea air instantly assaults my senses. Any other time, it would be quite lovely. It's been ages since I went to the beach, although I did read a fantastic romance book last week that was centred around summer holiday time and scuba diving in southern France.

My musings are interrupted by Mia taking my arm rather forcefully. She half walks, half drags me along as we follow Allegra toward what I think is a slipway. Turning my head, I desperately look for any sign of Kelley.

"She'll be onboard," Mia comments.

Seriously, can they all read minds?

A small-ish dinghy awaits us. Allegra steps onboard without so much as a look in my direction. She takes her place at the helm. I'm shoved to one of the seats at the rear. The only thing keeping me from a panic attack is the sight of Kelley, who is thankfully alive. She's conscious, too, although extremely pale.

The second she is in reaching distance, I pull her to my side. "Are you okay?"

Silly question, really. The woman has a hole in her shoulder. She nods silently, burying her head in my neck. There are no words, so I simply hold her. Guilt roils in my stomach. I should have insisted she go home; should have done more to keep my best friend safe.

The roar of the engine startles us both. There is still a kernel of hope this is all some overblown prank. But that kernel is getting smaller by the second. Mia and the other goons settle themselves on the boat. Allegra does a quick visual sweep of the dinghy before hitting the throttle. Everything about her is both impressive, and fear-inducing.

She's strong, both physically and mentally. It doesn't take a psychologist to figure that out. From her interactions with the others, she is well and truly the boss, but not the "big boss". No, she answers to someone—the someone who wants to see me. I have no idea what is going to happen, and for someone who likes routine, that makes me sweat. Maybe it will be as simple as a quick chat and soon I'll be on my way home with Kelley.

Unlikely.

Now the hysteria and shock have worn off, I know I need to be smarter. No more gobbing off at Allegra. That's a surefire way to get a hole to match Kelley's.

The best approach would be to sit quietly and take in as much as I can. I'll need all the information possible for the police. That's if they believe me, and I get out of this in one piece.

My gaze drifts to Allegra, who is standing tall, casting her intensity out to the open water. I think back to what she said earlier: that as soon as she drops me off, I'll never see her again. For some reason, that doesn't seem likely. In fact, I think I'm going to be seeing the blonde maniac quite a lot.

Strangely, the thought doesn't scare me.

4

Allegra

Ms Moorside is fascinating. Behind the copious amounts of wool is the heart of a fighter. She's lost her cool several times since we picked her up, and I like it. There is nothing hotter than a fiery woman.

Of course, it's highly entertaining watching her plot and plan. She has a useless poker face, but I admire her guts. I wonder if she would have followed through with her plan to get my gun.

The thought makes me chuckle. Thankfully, the wind covers any noise. I don't need anyone noticing my interest in the bookstore manager—or the fact she intrigues me.

I'd marked her as someone who would wither away under pressure—a meek mouse of a human. Sure, there was the vomiting incident, but she found her fire again, and quickly. It's like she can't stop herself from verbally hitting back.

As I said: Fascinating.

It irritates me some. I was ready to drop her off and never see her again, but now I want to know how she copes with Don Ferrante. He's an impressive man and makes the toughest of people cower. Somehow, I believe Ms Moorside will be as much of a surprise to him as she was to me.

My wait will be short-lived. The cliffside entrance to Don Ferrante's most secure residential option in the UK is coming up fast. The family staying here is the only reason I didn't push back harder against coming to Britain. Out of all his properties, this one is the safest, outside of Sicily.

The cliff looms over us as I bring the boat to a crawl. Without experience, a dinghy could easily become damaged on the sharp rocks that lay hidden beneath the high tide. I am the only one I trust to deliver the boat and its passengers safely. Some say I'm a control freak, and I wholly agree. There is a reason I am where I am in this life, and it comes down to trusting myself to get the job done. Don Ferrante is the only other living creature I trust.

Mattia is waiting for us on the small dock. Like all the staff, he dresses in all black.

"Good to have you home, Allegra," he says as we moor. "No problems?" he asks, eyeing Ms Moorside and Kelley.

I shake my head. "No. Where is Don Ferrante?"

"In his office. I radioed up. He's waiting."

Stepping off the boat, I don't look back. Mia and Toni will escort our guests. And for some reason, I'm reticent to see Ms Moorside's reaction to her surroundings. I'm not sure why. The woman means nothing to me, and yet, I have a vision playing on a loop in my head of her face when I shot her friend. The sheer terror, which I expected, is usually something I revel in, yet with her, it has conjured something else—something I'm not ready to explore. So, I will do my job, drop her off, and hope I'm finally told what this has been all about.

The stone steps leading up to the cellar are damp and cold. God, I hate the winter, especially outside of Italy. I can't wait to get home. Actually, I can't wait to get to my room to shower and change. Though I'm used to having my hair scraped back, it still gives me a pounding headache after several hours. Maybe I'll just chop it off.

Two guards wait at the cellar entrance. They give me a curt nod as I pass by. Leading the way through the main house, I almost stop to see what Ms Moorside makes of it all, but I catch myself in time. Show no weakness—no interest—that's how the head of a family should act.

Only when we approach Don Ferrante's office do I stop and turn. "Take Kelley to receive proper treatment," I say to Toni. "Mia, guard the door."

Toni whisks Kelley away. I can see Ms Moorside wants to run after her, but she's sensible enough to remain still. As soon as Toni and Kelley disappear around the corner, her gaze returns to me. There is that defiance again. It's like an ember that glows in her eyes, just waiting to ignite. I lick my lips and her eyes follow the movement. Interesting.

Mia, clearing her throat, brings me back to the task at hand. Turning, I take a second to breathe slowly, letting my impenetrable mask slip back into place. I knock once and then push the door open. Expecting Don Ferrante to be waiting behind his desk, I'm surprised to see him standing by the window, gazing out onto the garden.

"Sir, Ms Moorside," I announce.

Normally, I call Don Ferrante by his first name. But not in the company of a stranger. I show him the respect he deserves as the head of the family. Stepping to the side, I effectively expose Ms Moorside, who was hiding behind me. She's wringing her hands as her eyes dart around the room, finally landing on the Don. Her eyebrows furrow and I know she's desperately trying to figure out who he is.

"You may leave, Allegra," he says without turning around.

I grit my teeth. He's dismissing me. Ms Moorside turns slightly in my direction, and I can see she doesn't want me to go. After all, I am the devil she knows. The Don is an unknown threat.

Knowing better than to argue, I exit the office and quietly shut the door. My earlier desire to shower and change is gone. Now, I need to release some frustration. I hope Toni has dealt with Kelley because I need to beat on him for a few hours. Toni is one of the very few people brave enough to take me on.

"Stay here," I grind out to Mia as I leave. She's smart enough to keep her face passive.

Toni is just leaving the guest wing when I see him.

"All good?" he asks.

"Suit up. We're training."

Sweat pours from my brow. My breathing is laboured, but

I'm not done, unlike Toni, who looks seconds from collapse.

"Get up," I growl. Adrenaline is flowing and I feel antsy to throw some more punches. My body is going to protest in the morning, but I don't care.

"I'm done, Allegra," he gasps.

"I'll step in," Rosa says from the door. She's already got her hands wrapped. I nod and Toni crawls off the mat.

"Do your worst," I say, jumping up and down to loosen up.

Rosa smiles at me. She's just as vicious as me, but lacks my stamina. I train constantly. If I'm not in meetings or taking care of business in other ways, I'm in the gym. Every property has one. I ensure all the staff and family members are trained in several martial arts. It's the main reason other families fear us so much. The days of old are just that—old. So many families still live by an outdated way of life. The head of the family sits, getting rich and fat, relying on their position to scare workers into submission. They expect their underlings to do all the dirty work and fighting, leaving themselves weak.

In this family, it is expected every member, be they a driver, cook, or, like me, a boss, will be capable of deadly force. We all know we can take care of business. It bonds us as a family, too. There is a hierarchy, like other mafia families, but we are different. There is no need to use fear, not when each person under the umbrella of the Ferrante name wants to be here because they love the Don, and me, and each other. We strive for pure loyalty. They know their worth, as do I.

Rosa circles me several times. She's like a caged tiger ready to attack. Unfortunately for her, she's too easy to anticipate. Her eyes give her away, so the second she pounces, I am all over her. She fights with everything she has, which is precisely what I need to finally work through my frustration. Rosa lies on the mat, breathing heavily. I lay beside her.

"You were extra worked up today," she splutters.

"Mmm."

"He will tell you," she says. "Patience."

Rosa is possibly the only other person, apart from Don Ferrante, who I can talk with honestly. I trust her to a point, like everyone else in the world. I keep a part of myself locked away. I know it's a way to protect myself. I learned from an early age to expect heartache. She is also my ex-lover. We have been intimate, and that builds a deeper bond.

"I know," I reply. "I'm going to shower. Thank you for this."

"Anytime."

I need to get showered and presentable quickly. The Don could call for me at any moment, and I want to be prepared for what's to come. Ms Moorside is important—more important than I realised. It's the only reason Lorenzo is keeping me at bay. There, I said his name. I fulfilled my task; therefore, I'm back at my rightful station as Lorenzo Ferrante's heir.

We need to talk. I have to air my frustration at being kept out of the loop. No matter how hard I try, I can't shake the disappointment. I've worked too hard to be so easily demoted. And that's what the task felt like: a demotion. There was no reason Lorenzo couldn't have sent Mia and Toni alone. Was he sending me a message? I detest questioning myself like this.

I've just fastened my belt buckle when I receive a summons. Instead of my tight bun, I let my hair flow freely. I'm in all black again, but instead of combat trousers, I opt for slacks; Italian made, of course. My black silk shirt feels good against my skin. The clothes are my armour. I feel strong and in control when I wear my "Boss" attire. It might sound ridiculous, but sometimes perception is everything.

Knocking on the office door once more, I don't wait to enter. This time, Lorenzo is behind his desk. Ms Moorside is nowhere in sight.

"Take a seat, Allegra," he says in his commanding, yet comforting tone. "Drink?"

We often share a glass of brandy. I nod and he sets about pouring two doubles. Sitting silently, I keep my composure, just waiting for him to sit and explain.

We both take a sip of our drink, allowing the silence to descend. I learned everything I know from this man, so it's not a shock he can out-wait me by miles. I grin at myself as I lose the game. "Okay, are you ready to tell me what is going on?"

He chuckles, "Still can't beat my patience I see, my dear."

"Lorenzo."

He holds up his hand in a placating manner. "I appreciate your professionalism, as usual. I know you've wanted to question me from the second I gave you the order to find Bonnie."

He is referring to her by her first name. Interesting.

"I'm confused, Lorenzo. Toni and Mia could have gone to collect her. I'll be honest, it felt like a punishment. Have I displeased you? Offended you in some way?"

"Allegra, there is nothing you could do to displease me. You run this family honourably. Every decision you make is for the good, and the longevity, of the Ferrante name."

"Then please explain. Who is Ms Moorside? Why was it so important *I* get her?"

He empties his tumbler before answering. "Bonnie is my daughter."

5

Bonnie

DOING A MENTAL TALLY of how many books I've read this year is the only way to stop myself from slipping into hysteria—again. I refuse to be the stereotypical damsel in distress. My leg bounces as I wait for someone to take me to Kelley. The demand was my only response when the crazy man in the big office told me I was his daughter.

His daughter!

I have no clue who Lorenzo Ferrante is. I never heard of him in all my years. According to my dads, they never received the name of my birth parents. Now I'm questioning the truth of it all. But even if they knew, I can't blame them for keeping that kind of information from me, because from what I've witnessed so far, the man is definitely on the wrong side of the law. He is the textbook depiction of a mafia boss. If I think of every mob boss I've come across in books, Lorenzo Ferrante fits the bill to a T.

And then there's Allegra. A typical henchwoman; all moody and scary. She could probably kill me with one of her icy glares. I bet grown men wet themselves when she's in a bad mood. I'll save the fact the thought kind of turns me on, for the therapy sessions I will absolutely need after this. How quickly does Stockholm Syndrome develop?

I'm rambling in my own head. There aren't enough anti-anxiety meds in the world to combat this meltdown. Maybe singing "The Bottle Song" will help.

Ninety-nine green bottles sitting on the wall.
Ninety-nine green bottles sitting on the wall.
And if one green bottle should accidentally fall.
There'll be ninety-eight green bottles sitting on the wall.

Nope, still having a meltdown, just with an annoying earworm for company. Fantastic.

A grandfather clock chimes right next to me and I almost hit the roof. I've been so lost in my panic-ridden thoughts and unhinged bottle-singing, I blanked out my surroundings. So much for observing and cataloguing information for the police.

God, I'd make such a crap main character in a mafia book. My thoughts stray to *Mob's Seduction*. I still hate the title. I think about how strong the lead character is; the one that's forced to marry the mob queen and how very unlike her I am. Damn, I wish I'd thought to put it in my bag now. Maybe I could have picked up a few tips and tricks. I need all the help I can get. Let's be honest—I'm so screwed.

Mia steps up next to me and tips her head, which I'm guessing means I have to follow her. Lorenzo said he would have me taken to Kelley straight away, but it's been at least twenty minutes. Clearly, I don't get my impeccable punctuality from him. Blimey, that's something else to analyse later. I can't process family traits right now.

I know, being on a first-name basis with a mafia boss is a bit odd, but that's what he told me to call him. And honestly? *Don Ferrante* feels even weirder.

I follow like a good captive. No need to rock the boat. I'm sure all these people are bonkers, and the last thing I need is to piss off Mia and end up fish food. I wonder if they really do that? You know, tie blocks to peoples' feet and throw them in the water?

As if this is the time to be wondering that! Focus, Bonnie!

The stately home we're now wandering is...well, stately. Everything looks antique and expensive. I couldn't tell a Picasso from a hole in the wall, so I'll just presume the many, *many* paintings are expensive, too. Mia takes me up a grand set of stairs. I'd be impressed if I weren't so frightened.

After passing several doors, she finally leads me into a room at the end of the upstairs hallway. Kelley is sitting up in bed eating a sandwich, laughing at some woman who is tending to her shoulder.

Rushing past Mia, I practically throw myself at my best friend. She hisses in pain but holds me tightly. "I'm okay," she says.

"I'm not," I sob. I am far from okay. Pulling back, I give her a thorough scan. Her colour is back, and she has mayonnaise round her mouth. All-in-all, she looks great, which is baffling because doesn't she realise what's happening?

"I'll leave you to it," the still-unknown woman says. "I'll be back later to change the dressing, Kel. Rest up."

Kel?

Kelley smiles. "Thanks, Beth."

If I'm not mistaken, there's a twinkle in my best friend's eye. Mia follows this Beth lady outside and shuts the door. I hear the distinctive sound of the lock engaging. No way we can make a run for it, then.

"We're in so much trouble, Kelley."

"Yeah, so what's going on?" she casually asks, taking another bite of her sandwich.

"Kelley, how are you not freaking the hell out? And where did you get that?" I ask, pointing at the aforementioned sandwich. It smells divine.

"Want some? It's excellent. Beth made it for me. Isn't she dreamy?"

Taking Kelley by the face, I level her with the best "I'm-not-messing-about" stare. "Kelley, we've been kidnapped by mobsters. Beth is a mobster."

"A dreamy mobster," she sighs.

"Have they drugged you?"

She was a blubbering mess when Allegra came into the shop earlier. Why is she not a wreck now?

"No, and I get that we're in a shitty situation. I wish Blondie hadn't shot me. But then again, I wouldn't have met Beth, who I think might be my soulmate."

I narrow my eyes because I can't believe my ears. Kelley, my best friend, who thinks buying a different brand of tea bag is too much drama to handle, is sitting here, casually chatting about a mobster being her true love. Maybe she's in shock. I've heard that does strange things to a person.

"I'm going to bypass everything you've just said because it's crazy—just as crazy as meeting the man behind our abduction, who, according to him, is my father."

Kelley chokes on her latest chunk of sandwich, which is a much more appropriate response than the one I got a few seconds ago.

"Your *father*?"

Now I know Kelley is okay, I can't keep the last hour at bay any longer. "Yes. His name is Lorenzo Ferrante. And apparently, he gave me up to protect me and my mother."

"Whoa, back up there, lady. Take it from the top. What happened after we got separated?"

Unbuttoning my cardigan because I am unbelievably warm, I shake the thought of Allegra from my mind. Why she keeps popping up like a damn mole, I have no idea. Kelley wants me to recall the meeting with Lorenzo, and all I can do is picture Allegra's unique eyes boring into me.

"Earth to Bonnie?" Kelley waves a hand in front of my face.

"Right, yeah. Okay, so Allegra—crazy blonde lady—took me to see Lorenzo."

"What does he look like?"

"Well, me, I guess." I don't want to think about how his hair is the same shade as mine, or how even his chocolate-brown eyes are the same hue and same almond shape, or how he smiles a smile I see in the mirror every day. "He's tall."

"The details are astounding," Kelley deadpans. "Describe him to me like you would a character from a book."

"But he isn't a character, Kel. He's supposedly my dad."

Ugh, I don't like how that word sounds. I have two fabulous dads who are loving and kind and most definitely not criminals. Lorenzo is nothing more than a sperm donor.

"Okay, we'll skip the description. What did he say?"

I think back to sitting in the room with a man that both scared and intrigued me; a stranger looking at me with wonder in his familiar eyes—but a stranger, nonetheless. I couldn't relate to him in any way, so I sat there silently as he spoke. I sat there as he told me how he'd met my mother and fallen in love, but she was his mistress. And how, if my existence had been revealed, I would have been hurt in the name of retribution. His wife was the unforgiving type, apparently.

He had me and my mother sent away, but his plan didn't foresee my mother dying during labour. He arranged a closed adoption for me, and as a result, my ties to Lorenzo Ferrante were severed, all in the name of keeping me safe.

"Holy shit balls! That's intense, Bonnie."

"Ya think!" Finally, she's on the same page as me.

"And then what happened?" I'd find Kelley's enthusiasm funny if this weren't about my life.

"He said a rift between him and another family is the reason he needed to see me. They found out he had a daughter and threatened to kill me and my dads."

"Jesus. This is like *Mob's Seduction*, Bonnie. We're, like, living a fictional mob story right now!"

"I wish you wouldn't seem so happy about it, Kel."

"I wasn't in the beginning. I was terrified."

"And now you're *not*?" I screech. "Kelley, look around. This is really happening. We're being forced to stay here by people who are most likely murderers. This is insane!"

"But it's an adventure, right? I mean, Pete would think this is just what we need to live a little. He's been on you for months to get out of the apartment."

"I highly doubt this is what he was thinking. Christ, Kelley, are you that blinded by Beth's pretty face?"

"It is pretty, isn't it?"

Yes, Beth is pretty. Not the point, though, right? What the blazes am I going to do? I thought I'd be in here plotting ways to escape with Kelley, not listing ways to convince her to leave after she's fallen in love with one of our captors.

"Oh my God," Kelley suddenly blurts, "you're a princess!"

Okay, now I know she's not right in the head. A concussion! That's the only explanation for this shit show.

"I'm not a princess. I'm a bookstore manager being kept against her will by criminals, as are you, and we need to get out of here."

"You're not going anywhere until Don Ferrante says so." That voice. It sends chills down my spine and fire through other parts of me. I didn't even hear the door open. Kelley isn't looking so pumped about our situation now.

Looking over my shoulder, I grit my teeth. "You have no right to keep me here," I shoot back with as much venom as possible. I won't let her see how scared I am. Fuck her, and fuck Don Ferrante.

"And you have no choice. You might be his heir, but I won't hesitate to kill you if you so much as breathe wrong. Is that clear?"

Wow, I didn't think she could get any colder towards me, but I was mistaken. There is fury rippling off her in waves, and it's all directed at me. I've never met someone who hates me. Strong dislike, yeah, but nothing compared to the hatred Allegra is shooting my way.

Swallowing, I stand from the bed. Kelley's hand reaches for mine in a silent show of support. "I'm sure Dear Old Dad wouldn't appreciate that," I scoff, "so don't go throwing around useless threats, Allegra."

Oh, boy, that was the wrong thing to say.

Out comes the gun again. "You're right," she sneers, "but then again, I don't have to kill *you* to get my point across. Isn't that right, Kelley?"

Shielding Kelley with my body, I stare Allegra down. "I don't know what your damage is, and frankly, I don't care. I want nothing to do with you or Lorenzo, or this damn family. Is that clear? I just want to go home."

"And I've told you, that isn't happening."

"We'll see about that." I *will* get out of here.

"Bonnie," Kelley says quietly, "maybe here is the best place." I whip round to stare daggers at my friend's utterly ridiculous statement. "I—if there is someone out there who wants to hurt you, maybe staying here *is* the best option," she rushes to add.

"If it were up to me," Allegra interjects, "I would leave you to fend for yourself. But it's not, and the Don wants you here, safe. Accept it and adapt, Ms Moorside."

Accept and adapt. Right, sure, no problem.

Ha!

6

Allegra

THERE ISN'T MUCH THAT shocks me. I've seen far too much in my life for things to knock me off balance. Today, however, I am shocked—and angry. I've given everything to Lorenzo—all my trust and loyalty—and yet he hasn't afforded me the same courtesy. Keeping such information from me, after I've shared everything with him, is a betrayal in my eyes; one I never thought possible from him.

I sat there as he tried to explain away his reasons for keeping me in the dark, but none of them suffice. I've stolen and taken beatings. I've killed for him. I've done it all because he is the closest thing I have to a father. But he isn't my father, he's Bonnie Moorside's.

He knows I'm angry. But that didn't stop him from asking a favour of me; a favour I had zero inclination to take on. But then he looked at me in that proud parent way and I wilted. Lorenzo is my only family, and even though I am furious, I can't deny him his request. It's why I am here, outside Kelley's room, readying myself to go in and talk with Bonnie.

It doesn't go to plan though because *of course* she's plotting to run away and *of course* we exchange heated words. There is something about the wool-clad woman that both infuriates and excites me. She looks so weak, but her streak of fire is never far from igniting. I can see the fear in her eyes, even though she's too proud to let it show elsewhere. Well, I see her fear, and that is what I'll use to keep her in line.

Lorenzo asked me to look after her. Keep her safe. Try to teach her to defend herself. It's a laughable task because we both know Bonnie wants nothing to do with me or him. As she shouted at me seconds ago, she just wants to go home.

I wonder if she realises I'd love to go home, too. Back to Sicily, where none of this exists. I want to be in the villa looking out over our vineyard, taking care of important business, not babysitting a woman who is going to do everything in her power to make my life hell.

I've told Bonnie to accept and adjust. That's advice I need to take myself, because I know I won't go against

Lorenzo's wishes. I'll do my job even though it will be taxing, and frankly, below me. I guess the Don's plan to step back and retire is also on hold. I can't watch his daughter twenty-four seven and run the business. It's a clusterfuck all around, in my opinion. One giant step back for me and him.

A part of me wishes I'd argued with him instead of sitting there silently. I should have told him to look after the damn woman himself. It's what he deserves. His actions have turned our world upside down—ripped the curtain back on a truth Bonnie clearly didn't want to know. Me either, for that matter.

She stands with hands on hips, glaring at me. "What about my dads?"

"What about them?" I keep my tone level, hoping to seem unaffected by her. I'm pissed at myself that her existence even registers on my radar, let alone irks me.

"They're in danger too. We need to get them...bring them here!"

"Not my problem." God, I wish that were true. But I can see what's about to transpire. Bonnie will throw a fit and the Don will cower to her. Bonnie makes him weak. I can see it in his eyes. He wants to be the father she never knew; the father he craved to be. Now I know why he took me under his wing. I was a cheap replacement for the daughter he had to give away.

"How can you be so cold?" she replies incredulously. "What if this were your family?"

I want to sneer at her and tell her my family is gone, but I have some shred of self-control left. She doesn't deserve my life story.

"I'll talk to Don Ferrante." It's the only thing I can think of saying. I purposely call him by his title. To call him Lorenzo in front of her feels too intimate. It's a part of our lives she doesn't deserve. Bonnie might be his bastard child, but she's a stranger not worthy of our respect or loyalty. That's earned through sweat and blood. Bonnie has shed neither for this family.

"Thank you," she says with a little less venom.

"Don't thank me. I couldn't care less what happens to you or your family. I do what the Don asks. Nothing more. You are not in charge here, Ms Moorside. Remember that."

I internally wince at the lie. I don't want to give a shit about her. I want to mean what I said about being happy to leave her to fend for herself or being more than willing to kill her, but I don't, and it makes me even angrier at the entire situation.

I place my gun back in its holster. Bonnie is staring at me strangely and I hate that it makes me self-conscious. Casting a quick glance at my chest, I make sure there isn't a button open or a stain on my shirt. I see nothing. Flicking my eyes up, I see what she was looking at. Interesting. It seems Ms Moorside is a fan of my cleavage. The smirk is instantaneous, and she knows I've caught her looking.

"You need to follow me," I say as she darts her eyes about the room, her cheeks reddening.

"Where? Why?"

"I'm to show you to your room, Ms Moorside." *Like a fucking lapdog.* "It's late and you need rest."

"I want to stay here with Kelley," she shoots back. I sigh internally, because of course, she has to argue. Stepping forward, I have her over my shoulder before she registers my movements. It doesn't take her long to start screaming and beating my back with her fists, demanding I put her down.

Glaring at Kelley, warning her not to do anything stupid, I swivel around and march out of the room with an apoplectic Bonnie. I'm tired and want to relax before sleeping. My mental fortitude is waning and I cannot deal with her dramatic shit right now. We'd still be arguing in Kelley's room if I hadn't taken action.

Bonnie might be small, but she's no pushover. I have to considerably tighten my grip to keep her in place as I ascend the stairs to the second floor. Kicking the door open, I dump her off my shoulder and onto her bed. "Your room. Good night."

I want to laugh as I watch her scrambling to get to her feet. "You can't just manhandle me," she screams.

I'm in front of her in a second with my hand wrapped around her throat. "I can do as I please. This is my family, my house, and my rules."

She narrows her eyes in defiance. "Is it your house? Your rules?"

Gritting my teeth, I lean even closer. My lips are millimetres away from hers. "Yes, it is. Don't be fooled. I am the head of this family."

Her retort is instantaneous and cold. "No, Allegra, you're a replacement."

The wind is knocked from my chest. I've underestimated her. She has a cruel streak, just like her father. I'm a little proud, to be honest. She isn't cowering. In fact, I think she's even surprising herself if her wide eyes are anything to go by. She's not used to delivering such cutting words.

"The door will be locked," I grit out. Shoving away from her, I stalk out of the room, filled with emotions I have no business feeling. Why is my usual composure failing around her? I've dealt with the worst of human society and none of their remarks have ever hit their targets. I don't care enough about them to let their words affect me. But Bonnie's have. They've hit a painful bullseye.

Deep down, I know why. As cold and ruthless as I am—as I want the outside world to believe—I crave what can never truly be mine. Lorenzo took me in and treated me like his own, but the hard truth is I'm not, and I never will be. However, I have worked my ass off to get where I am today, and no one is going to take that away from me. Being a replacement is enough. I can live with that. There is no other choice.

My room is opposite Bonnie's. I wish now I'd locked her in elsewhere. How can I relax when she is so close? She makes me want to storm back in and scream at her. This waif of a woman has well and truly gotten under my skin.

"You look like you want to murder someone," Rosa says, rounding the corner, heading to her own chamber.

She is the answer to my prayers. I need to distract myself from the past few minutes, and what better way than sex? Rosa and I have not fucked in a while, but I think it's time to break the seal once more. We both know it will be nothing more than a release.

"My bed," I growl. Her pupils dilate and she licks her lips. She takes a final step towards me and claims my mouth roughly. Lust takes over, and instead of dragging her into my room, I spin her and slam her against Bonnie's door.

"Fuck me, Allegra," Rosa gasps.

Dropping to my knees, I rip her pants down until they pool at her feet. Rosa's hands grasp at the door, looking for something to hold on to. I waste no time plunging my tongue into her wet folds. She's ready for me, and I need this. Maybe it's my sadistic side that wants Bonnie to listen to me fucking another woman against the door that holds her captive. Or maybe it's my way of demonstrating the power I have; the power she just stripped from me with a few callous words.

Whatever my reasoning, Rosa is panting and slamming her hand rhythmically against the door as I take her closer to the edge. As she chants louder, I can't help but wonder what Bonnie is doing. Is she listening? Touching herself or curled up on the bed, plugging her ears? My gut says the former, however. She'll hate herself for feeling turned on. I saw it in her eyes when she stared at my tits. Here is my opportunistic revenge. She made me feel out of control, so now I'm returning the favour.

"Fuck, Allegra. That was something else." Rosa slumps against the door, her face red and her breathing laboured. "Please tell me I get a turn."

"Go to my room," I say, my voice slightly breathless. Rosa will think it's because I'm turned on and in need. But the truth is, I lost myself to thoughts of Bonnie Moorside.

Rosa practically skips to my room, and I know I'll follow, but I need a moment. I'm still facing Bonnie's locked door and an irrational need to see her almost knocks me back to my knees.

Is she standing on the other side, straining to hear what's happening? Am I losing my fucking mind? A growl escapes my throat in sheer exasperation. What the fuck am I doing, getting all bent out of shape over a bookstore manager? A woman who could ruin the life I've so carefully curated.

Tearing myself away, I cast all thoughts of her to the back of my mind. It's the shock of learning who she is. That's the only rational explanation for feeling and behaving this way. I just need to recentre myself and concentrate on what matters. Yes, I'll make sure she comes to no harm, but that's it. She can stay locked away with her friend while I reestablish my position. Lorenzo and I are going to have another talk, and this time, *he* will do the listening.

I am Allegra Malgeri, for fuck's sake. Maybe it's time to remind my beloved Don of that. He knows what I'm capable of. He knows what I have done and sacrificed for him and this family. There is no Ferrante legacy without me at the helm.

7

Bonnie

MY BODY IS STILL flooded with adrenaline after my altercation with Allegra. Maybe it was the way she threw me over her shoulder like a sack of spuds, or maybe it was the argument afterwards that still has me vibrating with pent-up anger. It's definitely *not* the fact she clearly just did rather adult things with someone, up against my door.

The woman is awful. I understand why Lorenzo has her running his evil empire. She's well-suited for it. A pang of regret burns in my stomach. I was equally awful in our last exchange. I like to think I'm a good person. I go out of my way to make people's days pleasant. Growing up, my dads often said I was too nice. I don't feel like that nice little girl right now.

I intentionally hurt Allegra. I don't know where it came from, but I knew it would wound her. I saw a vulnerability and exploited it to cause her pain. Some might say it was deserved. After all, she's kidnapped me, shot my best friend, and threatened to kill me. But aren't I just as bad if I retaliate?

The fact I could be so cutting is a concern, too. Naturally, I'm wondering if I've inherited some less than savoury characteristics from Don Sperm Donor. It's not just brown hair and brown eyes that have been passed on, it seems.

Gah! This kind of pondering should be done over a tub of ice cream whilst hiding under a blanket on my couch, not in the secret lair of my biological father.

Oh, my God, it sounds insane! If, and that is a big if, I get away, who in their right mind is going to believe me? I'd like to think Kelley would back up my story, but after her little display of dribbling over Beth, I'm not so sure now.

Okay, I need to ground myself. I'm quite new to yoga. I started practising last month and I'm honestly not sure I'm cut out for it. My body is more stout and rigid than lean and flexible. I do, however, enjoy the breathing exercises and the way they help me calm my anxieties.

Pete said yoga only counted as a hobby if I went to an actual class rather than trying to learn on my own in my apartment. I chose to ignore his opinion. Back to the task at hand: processing the past twelve hours and figuring out what the hell I'm supposed to do.

I need to take a measured approach to my current situation. If I learned anything from my parents, it's how to step back, organise my thoughts, and then make an action plan.

I sit on the floor with my legs crossed, doing my best to look like a seasoned yogi. Closing my eyes, I breathe deeply and focus on my energy. Once I feel in a state of relative calm, I collect my jumbled thoughts and start to unpack them.

First point to analyse: being kidnapped and watching Kelley get shot. It was harrowing, but all in all, I think I handled myself well. It would have been a mistake to try to get Allegra's gun, so in a silver lining sort of way, I'm pleased she was able to read me so easily and get me to see the stupidity of it. If not, I might be dead in a ditch now, probably because I shot myself. I have no idea how to use a gun.

Watching Kelley get hurt will require some professional help, but I am a master at compartmentalising, so I'm confident I can shove that to the back of my mental closet for now. The most important thing is Kelley is okay…sort of. Her mental state is somewhat questionable right now.

Moving on: Lorenzo Ferrante is my biological father, and I've got some pretty nasty people after me because he's a crime family boss. I never thought about my bio parents. My dads *were* and *are* great parents. I had everything I could ever want, not just materially, but emotionally, too. Why would I need to seek out people who didn't want to keep me?

The problem is, now I know it wasn't such a straight-forward situation. On the other hand, Lorenzo chose his horrible wife over me and my mother. Surely, with all his power, he could have found a different way to handle the mess he created. I suppose it's neither here nor there any-more. He gave me away, and that's that. Going forward, though, I'm not so clear as to where my feelings stand.

By all accounts, he and his merry band of criminals are all terrible human beings. There's no rational reason I should want anything to do with them, but something inside of me is curious. I suppose it makes me wonder what my life would have been like if he'd kept me. Would I be as ruthless and heartless as Allegra?

My guess? Yup, that's definitely what would have happened. After all, Lorenzo took *her* in and groomed her to be the perfect mafia queen. It doesn't take a qualification in psychology—which both my dads have—to guess how she ended up connected to Lorenzo. If I *have* to guess, I'd say Allegra has no parents and Lorenzo has been her surrogate dad. That's why my last words to her were so cruel.

Stop thinking about Allegra.

Right—back to Lorenzo and him being my father. Maybe if we'd met under different circumstances, I'd be more open to getting to know him. But even with a curious mind, I can't forgive what he's done. Or can I? I need to table this conundrum for a different time. There's *way* too much to process and consider. Right now, I need to stick to the smaller things.

Changing my train of thought leads me to my current predicament: being locked away in this gigantic and admittedly gorgeous—if you're into antiques—room. Everything in me wants to run away. But if Lorenzo is telling the truth, I could be in more danger if I leave. Staying put would be the sensible course of action, right?

What about the bookstore, though? Surely, Clive will realise I'm missing. It's not like Janice will really give a shit, but even she will see the store isn't open and will wonder where I am... I think. Plus, I ring my dads every night without fail, unless they know I have a new book to read—like *Mob's Seduction*—so actually, they won't be expecting me to call until at least tomorrow. That might be a good thing, though. It gives me time to talk to Lorenzo about them. I don't trust Allegra to pass on my demand to get them here. There is no way I'm leaving my parents to get hurt. They didn't ask for this, just as much as I didn't.

Alright, I'll not do anything daft tonight. I'll try to get some sleep, then demand to see Lorenzo in the morning, and have him secure my parents and call Clive. Okay, that's a solid plan.

Yoga meditation for the win!

Last but not least: Allegra. How am I going to deal with her? She's clearly the head honcho around these parts. By all accounts, Lorenzo is the only one above her, which means I'll have to interact with her whether I like it or not.

She's the mafia queen and I'm the unsuspecting civilian thrust into her world. I knew reading so many books would come in handy one day. If I do the opposite of everything the main character would do, when faced with an alluring, yet dangerous, mafia nut job, I'll be fine.

There will be no forced marriages, no fake relationships to appease other mafia families—none of it. Plus, it's not like Lorenzo wants me to take over the family business, so Allegra shouldn't feel threatened. She'll be in her corner, and I'll be in mine, being careful not to piss her off to the point of homicide.

Now I have my brain in order and am confident in my decisions, I need to get some rest. Actually, I need a shower because I feel gross. Wool and sea spray aren't a pleasant combination. Standing from my yoga pose, I try to will the blood to flow into my limbs again. Pins and needles are a bitch!

Shucking my skirt to the floor, I pick it back up and lay it over the back of the vanity chair. That's right—the room has a vanity desk that looks like something Queen Victoria would have used. Everything is so bloody old. I mean, it's lovely if you want to live in a museum, and I'm sure—like the paintings—the vanity costs an arm and a leg... but jeez, it's so dark and dowdy.

Once I've removed all my clothing and organised them neatly to prevent creases, I proceed to the ensuite. The gold is blinding: taps, plug holes, showerhead—everything is garish; however, the size of the shower cubicle makes up for the gaudy décor. There's also a claw foot bath I may utilise at some point. Might as well make the most of it, I guess.

The water feels heavenly against my skin. The journey by boat left me covered in a fine layer of salt. At least my tights kept my legs from the same fate. It's nice to release my hair from the low pony I usually wear. Running my hand through my locks makes me instantly think of Allegra and her super tight bun. Although she didn't have her hair up when she hauled me over her shoulder. It was flowing freely, and I'll admit, it did something to me when I first clapped eyes on her again. I've never seen natural platinum before. The light kept catching it and reflecting off it in an almost blinding display. She looked different, too. She's definitely more imposing in black silk.

Of course, I then think of the noises I heard outside the room. At first, it disgusted me. Not because the two women were having sex—I'm all aboard for that—it was Allegra's utter disregard for decency. I can't understand what point she was making. Did she want me to know how powerful she is? That she can have whomever she wants, whenever she wants? I guess that would make sense after what I said. Clearly, she needed to feel in control again. She probably wanted to banish the truth behind my coarse words: She is a replacement. I still feel shitty for saying that.

Or...and I'm not sure if this is wishful thinking... Did she want to... I don't know...turn me on? Did she want to let me know she is also a member of the rainbow family? But why would she? It's pretty clear she detests me. And more importantly, why do I enjoy the idea of her trying to turn me on?

See, this is where I need to remind myself of the books I've read. Having naughty thoughts about the mafia queen is like number one on the plotline list of things I need to avoid. Easier said than done, though. I might be the world's most boring person, but I still have carnal urges and functional eyeballs.

I roll my eyes because I can hear Pete's mocking tone in my head as he repeats *carnal urges* back to me with a grimace. It's times like this, when I use words like that, he thinks I'm one cat away from living as a spinster. He could be on to something.

Shaking my head, I surge on with scrubbing myself clean. That is, until I clean a certain body part and I realise Allegra succeeded, even if she didn't mean to. The mafia boss has turned me on.

Bloody marvellous. I'm already failing. Nothing I can do about it now. I just need to be extra vigilant going forward. No more thoughts about Allegra and what her mouth can do...or those long fingers.

Dammit.

8

Allegra

THE EXTRACURRICULAR ACTIVITIES DID their job. I woke refreshed and ready to put everything that happened yesterday behind me. Well, I still have the chat with Lorenzo to get through first.

Rosa left my room a little after 2 a.m. We were never the type to cuddle after sex. No reason it would start now. I slept well, and the second my eyes opened, I felt a fresh wave of determination roll over me. Bonnie might have gotten under my skin temporarily, but no more. My plan is to get back to work.

I feel invigorated after a fast five-mile run on the treadmill. I wish I could go outside and run through the lanes, but it isn't safe. I'll save that for Sicily. The scent of the vines is much more appealing than cow shit, anyway.

Showered and dressed to kill, I march to Lorenzo's office, where I know he will be. I forego knocking. I'm too revved up to be polite. His gaze snaps up as I barge in unannounced. As usual, though, he is a master of schooling his features.

Sitting opposite, I cross one leg over the other. I'm not here to play patient games with him. It's time to have my say.

"Yesterday was unacceptable, Lorenzo. I deserved better than that." He opens his mouth to protest, but I cut him off. "I have earned my spot at the top of this family tree. It might be your name, but it's my management that has kept this family going. I have given you every ounce of trust and loyalty, yet you don't offer me the same in return. I am hurt."

Lorenzo has never heard me speak so candidly. I'm usually a fortress where my feelings are concerned, but after yesterday, I can no longer trust him to read the room. He should have known what Bonnie's appearance would mean and how it would affect me. And maybe he did. He just cared more about her, than me.

"I run every part of the business because you asked me to. Hell, you trained me to do this—to be your heir. Now you have Bonnie, but as far as I am concerned it changes nothing. She is a temporary blip. We both know she doesn't want anything to do with you or the Ferrante name. So I'll cut to the chase, and I apologise if this hurts, but Lorenzo, you need to hear it. If you have some delusion that your long-lost daughter will step up to claim her birthright, you are mistaken. And even if she does, I will fight her *and* you, every step of the way. I earned this."

We sit silently for a long time as Lorenzo contemplates my words. I don't mind; I want him to soak in every one of them. Finally, he sighs. It's a defeated noise I'm not used to hearing from him.

"You're right. You deserved better, Allegra. And I know you're angry, but I promise I have no intention of taking this family away from you."

"Why didn't you tell me? I've been dealing with the Arellos for years. How could you not tell me about Bonnie?"

He jerks an eyebrow at the use of his daughter's first name. I bite the inside of my cheek because I should have kept it professional. That's more than once I've used her first name.

"The secret just became too big. And painful, if I'm truthful."

I see the pain in his eyes and it does affect me. I love the man, and I've done everything in my power to keep him safe and happy. It hurts I can't stop him from feeling this pain.

"The truth is all I want, Lorenzo. We could have been keeping an eye out for her years ago. Or made sure the Arellos never found out. You left us vulnerable, and now we have a bigger issue."

He drops his head, and suddenly, he looks tired. There is a reason I am taking over. Lorenzo is done. He is mentally drained, and unlike in some families, he isn't scared to admit it. Instead of dragging the business into the gutter out of sheer stubbornness, he's handing over the reins to me.

"Is she okay?" he finally asks.

"She's a pain in the fucking ass! But she's got fire, Lorenzo, and a sharp tongue. I see you in her."

His eyes well with tears. "I could have known her...if I'd made the right choice."

"Fenza would have torn her to shreds if she'd found out."

Fenza Ferrante had been Lorenzo's wife; a woman feared by everyone, including yours truly. She was vindictive, even to those she supposedly loved. Bonnie and her mother would have both met a grisly end. It was only by the grace of God that Fenza got drunk one night and drowned in the bath, and Lorenzo finally got free of her.

It sounds unkind to speak ill of the dead, but Fenza was a demon in human form: twisted and cruel. Lorenzo had no choice but to enter into the marriage for the purpose of producing an heir. When it was revealed Fenza was barren, she became even worse. No one was safe from her ire.

As soon as she was gone, which was only a year and a half after Lorenzo sent his mistress and unborn child away, he was able to rebuild the family into what he wanted, not the vision his father dreamed of. Papa Ferrante was old school and wanted to keep the family business that way. Lorenzo saw the wisdom of change and appointed me as his beneficiary. I was only three when my parents were killed, and I became the adopted daughter of Lorenzo Ferrante. He literally trained me my entire life to become a leader.

"I should have had her taken care of long before," he mutters darkly.

"You would have started a war. Karma took care of Fenza, and you got to keep your hands clean."

"But I lost her. I lost my daughter."

I'll not lie. That was a stab to the heart. I have to get used to the reality that I'm not, and never was, good enough to own his heart like a real daughter.

"Yes, but she's here now, I suppose." I can't help the attitude that comes out.

He looks at me with his piercing eyes. "You are my daughter too, Allegra. I thought that was clear. I'd die for you, as I would Bonnie. You have made me so proud. Never doubt your place in this family and in my heart."

Getting into deep emotional conversations makes me uncomfortable. My skin feels itchy and I want to run out the door, but I know better. I'll keep my mask on and my body armour engaged.

"We need a plan, Lorenzo."

Lorenzo lets me bypass his last comment, which I'm grateful for. "We should go home," he says. "Easier to protect her from the villa."

I nod in agreement. "Yes, but she has a demand," I say with a roll of my eyes.

A sly grin pinches at Lorenzo's mouth. "And what was the demand?"

"She wants her dads brought in for their protection too."

"Done. I'll send Toni to collect them."

Sitting forward, I hold up my hand. "Lorenzo. We can't just haul her entire family to Italy."

"Why not? It's the best way to get her to cooperate, Allegra."

"And the best friend?"

"I didn't tell you to take her too," he shoots.

I growl, "You didn't tell me anything! Bring me the girl. That's all I got. If I'd have known, I would have handled it differently."

His shoulders drop, and he nods, "You're right. I know. I...I suppose you can ask the friend what she wants to do."

My eyebrows reach my hairline. "Just let her go? After I shot her?"

"You shouldn't have done that either," he chuckles.

"It was the only way to bring Bonnie to heel," I reply matter-of-factly.

"She isn't a dog, Allegra."

"You weren't there," I protest. "She's stubborn and difficult. I didn't have time to waste, so I did what was necessary. Anyway, it was only a flesh wound."

For some reason, he's eying me strangely. "So, she rankled you, huh?" he grins. "The big bad Allegra Malgeri?"

My scowl only makes him laugh harder.

"She scared me too, if I'm honest," he smiles. "She has her mother's temper."

"Huh, I thought she got it from you."

He shakes his head with a fond smile on his face. "No, Bonnie is all Maria."

I need to get us back on track. "I'll talk to Kelley and Bonnie. Once we're back home, we need a plan to end this shit with the Arellos. It's gone on too long and is now impacting us internally."

The Arello family is the second biggest family name in Italy. We are the first. There's been a fracture between Lorenzo and Giani Arello for decades. I've always thought it was over land claims, but something is tingling my bullshit sensor. Giani has no problems fucking with our shipments, but he's never tried to go after a family member. That means this current problem is very personal, and he wants to hurt Lorenzo beyond the scope of business.

"Giani won't stop, Allegra. You know what he's like."

I do, and I don't. I usually deal with his cocksure son, Gisto, who will become head of the family once Giani dies. The old man will never relinquish control. Only the finality of death will get him to loosen his restricting grip. I kind of feel sorry for Gisto. He isn't surrounded by love or by true loyalty. Giani rules through fear and anger. I've witnessed Giani's rage once before and it was directed at his son.

However, my sympathy only stretches so far. Gisto is a chauvinistic reptile ninety percent of the time. I've lost count how many times he's claimed to be the right man to set me straight. One day I'll accept his offer and laugh as his bravado shrivels to the size of his microscopic dick. Men like that are all the same. All talk, no follow-through. He wouldn't know what to do with a woman. God only knows how his wife copes.

Oh, that's right, she doesn't. Instead, she fucks his younger brother.

"Then we need to find a way. I can deal with our cargo getting hit. But we can't keep everyone safe if he's set his eyes on hurting the family that way. There are too many of us."

I might be Lorenzo's only heir. I'm not counting Bonnie, but we have many, many members of the family: nieces, nephews, cousins, aunts, uncles. Lorenzo and I would be devastated if anything happened to any of them, which again leads me to think Giani's vendetta is something much more than I've been told. If he wants to hurt us, there are already plenty of options. Instead, he's taken the time to track down Bonnie and her family. Giani wants to rip Lorenzo's heart out by hurting his daughter.

"Fine. But now, we concentrate on picking up Bonnie's parents and getting everyone to the villa in one piece."

I nod and stand. As much as I want to retreat to my chamber for the rest of the day, I know I have work to do. Business back home hasn't stopped, and there will be mountains of emails to sift through. We are also coming up to harvest time, and I've never missed one yet. I'll be damned if I miss this one. The vineyard is the only thing that brings me true peace.

First, I have to talk to Bonnie and Kelley; something I wholeheartedly do not want to do. I'm not so worried about Kelley. She still looks like she's going to pass out every time she sees me. But Bonnie? She's a different matter, especially after my performance with Rosa against her door. In the cold light of day, it was childish and below me. My only excuse is her words cut me deep.

After talking with Lorenzo, I need to take a different tack. Antagonising her will only drag this out longer. The quicker we get her and her family to safety, the quicker I can deal with the Arellos and we can get back to normal, and to where I will never have to see that infernal woman ever again.

9

Bonnie

IT'S THE BAJILLION THREAD count on the duvet and the feel of silk sheets underneath, that first reminds me I'm most definitely not at home. My own duvet cover is scratchy and my mattress, lumpy. This mattress is like floating on a cloud of marshmallows.

The second reminder is the godawful décor I'm currently staring at with my bleary eyes. Third...um, third, is a scary blonde staring at me with different-coloured eyes from the corner of the room.

"What are you doing in here?" I screech, pulling up the covers until they're tucked under my chin. I had to sleep nude because I haven't got my pyjamas.

Allegra looks entirely unfazed by my squawking. She simply continues to watch me from the wingback chair, one leg crossed over the other and her hands resting on her lap.

"I'd thought you'd be awake by now, trying to tunnel out of the house," she says.

I narrow my eyes. "I won't be that obvious," I shoot back, presuming we're skipping yesterday's confrontation.

"We need to talk. Get dressed and come to Kelley's room."

"Why?" So much for me keeping a low profile and not antagonising her.

She grits her teeth and flares her nostrils. I wait for the acerbic response, but it doesn't come.

"Please, just do as I ask." And then she stands gracefully, gives me one last sweeping look, and leaves.

My heart is pounding. I'd like to say it's from the surprise of finding someone watching me as I sleep, but I'm not sure that's the reason...at least not the entire reason. As much as Allegra is a foul specimen of a human being, her stare stirs something in me. My mind conjures a particular scene in *Mob's Seduction*. Dammit, that's how it starts! The protagonist gets sucked in by the mob queen and her sultry looks. She gets all flustered and starts to feel attraction, even though the mob queen is a real piece of work. Well, I'm not falling for it. Nope! Allegra can do sweepy looks and smouldering eye contact, but she won't break me.

Satisfied I can keep it in my knickers, I slip out of bed and quickly shower again. I still feel like I have half an ocean on my skin. For once, I'm not looking forward to putting on my wool skirt. After the feel of silk sheets on my skin, I know the heavy material of my clothes is going to be uncomfortable.

Walking to the ugly vanity, I stop and stare. I *can't* put my wool skirt on because it isn't where I left it. None of my clothes are. What the hell?

Turning in a circle, I search for my clothes. Is this Allegra's childish way of pissing me off? I thought she would be more the finger-snapping and kneecapping type than a stealing-a-girl's-clothes kind of mobster.

Just as my anger begins to rise, I spot a pile of clothes on a small table next to the wingback chair. Cautiously, and with an air of suspicion, I approach. Neatly folded on it is a dark grey pencil skirt and a ruby-red silk shirt. There is even underwear...of the lace variety.

I'm not sure how long I stand there staring, but it must be approaching at least ten minutes. Allegra will probably burst through the door any second and drag me to Kelley's room, because I am most definitely late.

Did Allegra leave these here? Is she seriously trying to dress me? What kind of control freak does that?

My fingernails dig into my palm as I get more and more agitated. I do *not* want to wear clothes picked out by her! How dare she? But what choice do I have? I mean, I could make a statement and waltz to Kelley's room in just the undies. But the idea of Allegra assessing my body isn't worth the anxiety or other feelings her stare elicits.

Begrudgingly, I slip on the clothes and hate myself for feeling really good in them. The floor-length mirror makes me pause because I don't look like myself at all. I look... Wow! I look pretty hot!

Instead of the usual low ponytail, I let my hair hang free. For no other reason than to give my scalp a break. It has nothing to do with wanting to look alluring, in any way whatsoever. But let's say that was partly the case; I'd be doing it for me. No reason I can't look sexy for myself.

Batting away my thoughts, I go to leave until I remember I'm barefoot. One quick look and I see a pair of high heels I'm sure will break my ankles. I have the stability of a baby giraffe in flats, let alone skyscraper shoes. Okay, they're not quite that bad. Maybe two inches? Still, that's higher than I'm used to.

Letting out a frustrated growl, I stomp over and put the blasted things on my feet. I hate Allegra has dressed me so well. Hate. It.

With my mood trapped between sour and strangely satisfied with the way my body looks, I do my best to walk smoothly to Kelley's room. Stopping outside her door, I fix my face into resting bitch mode and enter. Ignoring Allegra completely, and that bloody smug grin plastered to her irritatingly pretty face, I head straight for Kelley, who is looking at me like I'm an alien. Until she wolf whistles, and then I want to punch her.

"Whoa, looking good, Bonnie. Wowzer!"

"How are you?" I grit out. I know Allegra has still got her eyes on me, but I won't give her the satisfaction of seeing how much she's pissed me off.

"No way. We need to stay on topic. What's all this?" Kelley asks with a sweeping motion up and down my body with her non-injured arm.

"This," I say, "is a violation of my rights. Yet again."

Kelley's eyes dart between me and Allegra. "Um, okay. But as far as violations go, you look great."

I hear the quiet snigger from behind and choose to be the bigger person.

"Why have you summoned me here?" I ask, turning from Kelley to Allegra. "What more could you possibly want from us?"

Allegra's hair is back in its tight bun. Sad, really, because her hair looks gorgeo—

Stop it right now, Bonnie Moorside! My inner voice is right. I need to concentrate.

"Don Ferrante has agreed to collect your parents," she says. A rush of air leaves my body.

Oh, thank God.

"They will arrive later today."

"Thank you," I reply tersely. I want to throw myself at her and hug her to death for doing this for me. Honestly, I didn't think she would pass on my demand.

She gives me a small nod. "We have decided that for your safety and that of your parents, we must return to Sicily. Our villa is the most secure of all the family properties."

Um...what?

"Hang on a second. You can't just take us out of the country. We have lives... Homes... Pets!" I argue.

"You have no pets, Ms Moorside," Allegra calmly states.

"That's not the point... I... You... I refuse!"

She's doing that thing again, where she grits her teeth and flares her nose. I understand now it's her way of stopping herself from launching whatever scathing comeback is sitting on the edge of her tongue.

"If your parents agree, will you come willingly?"

This new, calmer Allegra is throwing me off balance. "They won't, so it doesn't matter."

Her eyes are steely. Not in colour, but in determination. "If they do, will you?"

I huff, "Fine."

There is no way either of my dads will go along with it, so it's a moot point.

Another small nod. Her attention turns to Kelley. "Don Ferrante is happy for you to go home, if that's what you want."

Yes! Kelley can get help. Why on earth is Lorenzo letting her go? It's clear from the crease between Allegra's eyes this isn't her decision. Rightly so, because Kelley will bring the full force of the law—

"I'm not going home. Where Bonnie goes, I go."

"Kelley," I begin, shocked she's being so idiotic.

"That's my decision, Bonnie."

"So be it," Allegra replies. "Beth will be in shortly to tend to your wound." Allegra's hands curl into fists. "I...I'd like to apologise for that," she says, gesturing to Kelley's shoulder. Her arm is strapped across her chest, but apart from that, she looks fine. "I shouldn't have—"

"Shot my best friend," I scoff. "No, you shouldn't have. In fact, you shouldn't have done any of this. So save your apologies. They mean nothing if you still intend to keep us against our will."

Allegra's eyes turn to me. Her heterochromatic irises twinkle as a ray of sunlight passes through Kelley's open curtains. "None of this was my decision. Trust me when I say you are not worth the headache; however, Don Ferrante has requested you're kept safe, and that's what I'll do. Maybe it would be wise for you to stop being so indignant and see the situation for what it is: A way to save your boring life. You will be back at your cosy bookshop soon, going home to eat your sad microwave meals, with your even sadder wool clothes for company. Don Ferrante may not have gone about this in the right way, but his heart is in the right place. Whether you like it or not, he is your kin and will treat you as such. So stop your whining and grow up."

"How dare—"

"You are being taken to a luxury villa in Italy. You and your parents will be kept safe whilst enjoying a life of pure comfort. I will take care of the people who are hellbent on hurting you and then you can go home."

"People are after me because of you and this wretched family," I shout. "You brought this on me and my parents, so don't start trying to pass yourself off as some sort of hero. You're a criminal!"

"That may be so. But I'm the only one who will stop you from getting a bullet in your head!"

A thick silence descends on the room. Kelley's hand on my arm snatches my attention from Allegra, who is shooting fire from her eyes.

"She's not wrong, Bonnie."

"Oh, for fuck's sake," I growl, "stop thinking with your vagina, Kelley. Beth is pretty, I get it, but she's a bloody criminal too."

Pulling her hand back, Kelley sits up. "I'll forgive that outburst because I know you're stressed," she begins. "My reason for agreeing with psycho over there has zero to do with Beth and you know it. I was high as a kite last night on some pretty great painkillers. Beth is lovely, but I'd never bet your life on a pretty girl. You know *that*, because you know *me*!"

My shoulders sag as I deflate. Of course I know that, and I feel bad for snapping. "I'm sorry, Kel. This is all…"

"Too much. I know. Believe me, I'm scared too. But the fact remains, there are people who want to hurt you. Going home out of sheer stubbornness not only endangers you, but also your parents and everyone around them. Think of the trip to Sicily as a holiday, okay? We're going to go spend some time eating great food and drinking wine in a gorgeous country."

"We *do* have excellent wine," Allegra murmurs. I shoot her a look that clearly states she needs to butt out. Her response is an eye roll.

My thoughts are no longer a picture of organised bliss. "What about work? Clive will—"

"He has been informed of your absence and compensated accordingly. There is no issue in that regard."

"Of course you've already called my boss," I sneer.

"We're on a tight schedule, Ms Moorside. Are we all on the same page now?"

Running my hand through my hair, I weigh up the options. Everything in me wants to rebel against Allegra. Sod Lorenzo, *she's* the one who pisses me off, and the thought of doing anything she wants makes me break out in hives. I have to think of my parents and Kelley, however. Their safety comes first.

"Fine," I say, but I'm not done. I take a step toward Allegra. When I'm forehead to chin, I look up. My voice is low, so only she can hear me, "But if you touch my things again without consent, I will gut you in your sleep."

Her eyes flash and her pupils dilate. She looks down at my lips and back up. Her tongue sneaks out and delicately traces her bottom lip.

"Duly noted... Bonnie."

10

Allegra

I'VE NEVER BEEN TURNED on by a death threat, but Bonnie's promise to gut me in my sleep still rattles around my head four hours later, and the low throb still beats its tiny drum, making me clench my thighs together.

I've since spent my time in my office, catching up on paperwork. Everything is fine. The business practically runs itself under my rule. I'll still be glad to leave this awful place, though. English Heritage décor is not my thing at all. It's dark and oppressive.

Lorenzo hasn't left his office yet, which would usually cause concern, but I suppose he needs time to adjust to Bonnie being in his life. My guess is he has a lot of old issues resurfacing and needs to be alone.

The radio crackles to life, signalling Bonnie's parents' arrival. I wonder if they're going to be as troublesome as their daughter. God, I hope not. Packing away the paperwork in my satchel, I call for Mia to box up the office. I want to leave as soon as humanly possible once Bonnie's dads are onboard.

I'm just about to make my way to the main hall wher. Lorenzo steps out and waves me over. "Will you ask Mark and Phillip to come here first? I know they'll be eager to see Bonnie, but I think we need to have a frank discussion before emotions cloud their judgement."

"I'll fetch them now."

Mark and Phillip stand, hand-in-hand, in the main hall. They look nervous but meet my eyes with a determination I've seen in Bonnie.

"Where is our daughter?"

I've studied Bonnie's life, so I know Phillip is the one addressing me. After my talk with Lorenzo, I did my own research. That's why I left my chat with Kelley and Bonnie until this morning. I wanted to have all the pertinent information before this shitshow went any further.

Phillip and Mark Moorside are both psychologists working at a prestigious university. Phillip is fifty-two with short dark hair, a titanium knee, and a penchant for cigars, which Mark dislikes.

Mark is fifty-four with black hair that's closely cropped because he is starting to go bald. He likes baking and wool cardigans. No surprise Bonnie has such awful taste in clothes. Together, they have a nice four-bed house close to Bonnie's apartment. They talk daily with their daughter and enjoy garden parties.

For all intents and purposes, they have a very vanilla life and are happy. I try to ignore the pang of jealousy, but it's hard. As much as this family is all I've ever known, as is the lifestyle, I admit I've wondered what it would be like to live a boring suburban life.

"Bonnie is with her friend. She'll be brought to you shortly. First, Don Ferrante would like to talk. Please follow me."

The mention of Lorenzo's formal title doesn't even elicit the smallest of reactions, so I know they are aware of him. The fact I'm still in the dark pisses me off. Considering Bonnie's adoption was closed, I'd like to know how Mark and Phillip are acquainted with Lorenzo. And why he's never told me? I know I've never met Bonnie's parents, so if they have had cause to interact, Lorenzo has kept it a secret from me.

They follow me down the hall and to the office. Lorenzo is pouring three drinks. I gesture for Mark and

Phillip to sit on the couch before moving to the drinks table and pouring a fourth tumbler of brandy.

"I'm staying," I say quietly. Lorenzo gives a small nod.

"I'm sorry we're meeting like this," Lorenzo says, his back still turned away from the two men. I slink over to the other side of the room and lean against the wall. "You know I never meant for this to happen."

Well, that answers my question then. They know each other.

"You promised we'd never have to meet, Lorenzo. You swore Bonnie would be safe."

Well, isn't that interesting? Not only do they know Lorenzo by name, but they seem to have an understanding of what this is, or should I say, *who* the Don is.

Taking a second to steel himself, Lorenzo shoots a quick look my way before turning around. "You're right. I've not kept my word, and you'll never know how sorry I am for that. But we have to look past my failure and protect Bonnie."

Phillip stands and begins pacing. "Who is threatening her?"

"Giani Arello," Lorenzo replies. I'm surprised he's being so open, to be honest. "He..." Another side eye at me. I'm not going to like what I hear. "He was Maria's fiancé."

I sling back the brandy in one gulp before heading back to grab the bottle. After everything I said yesterday, Lorenzo is still keeping important information from me. My blood is boiling, but I have to keep it under wraps for now. I'll beat the living shit out of something later.

Mark gently guides his husband back to the couch. "How do you plan on dealing with this, Lorenzo?"

"I will deal with it," I interject. "No harm will come to your daughter, I swear it. But we need your help. Bonnie is less than happy to be here. A fact I take responsibility for. The way we met was less than ideal, but I didn't have all the facts," I say, scowling at Lorenzo, who at least has the decency to look ashamed. "The truth is, to keep you safe, we need to take you to Italy. Bonnie is understandably quite angry and is fighting me all the way."

I see a smirk take over Phillip's face. "That's our Bonnie. She's never liked being told what to do."

"That may be so, but this time, I need her to fall in line. She's agreed to come to Sicily if you are on board."

Mark takes Phillip's hand. "And this is the only way?"

"It is," Lorenzo chokes. "I'm so sorry."

I've never seen Lorenzo cry, and the fact he has tears streaming down his face makes me want to scream with discomfort. As much as Lorenzo showed me love growing up, we were never very demonstrative.

"Our villa is like Fort Knox, but prettier," I say with a smile. "You'll all want for nothing. I'll deal with Giani as swiftly as possible."

Mark and Phillip exchange looks before nodding. "We'll convince her to play nice."

"You should probably know…" Ugh, why do I care what these people think? "Kelley was injured. I sort of shot her."

I don't know why I'm explaining myself. I'd never dream of doing it with anyone else, but something in my gut tells me I need to be honest with them.

Mark's eyes go wide, and Phillip stands back up. "You did what?"

Lorenzo stands next and holds his hands up. "It's my fault."

"No, *I* shot her. All I can say is I didn't know who Bonnie was. She was planning to escape when we picked her up, and to teach her a lesson, I shot Kelley."

"Jesus Christ," Mark gasps.

"I apologised," I say somewhat meekly.

"And you want me to entrust my daughter's life in *your* hands?" Phillip barks.

"Yes," I state. "I will never hurt Bonnie." Those few words cause an avalanche of emotion I've never experienced before to slam into my stomach.

"Allegra is the best at her job. She protects the family at all costs, and Bonnie is—albeit reluctantly—a part of it. Please, Phillip, this really is all my fault."

Phillip scrubs his face. "I want to see her! Now!"

The talking portion of the day is over. I'm not sure if they will still help convince Bonnie to come with us or not. I should have probably kept my mouth shut, but then again, I'm sure Bonnie will waste no time informing her parents of how beastly I am.

Leading them out of the office, I take them to Kelley's room, where Bonnie remained after refusing to leave.

"I really am sorry," I say before pushing the door open.

Bonnie lets out a sob and runs into her dads' arms. I watch from the doorway at the outpouring of love. It's too much. I need to be anywhere but in this room. Turning, I head to the gym. Rosa is in the ring with Toni. She sees me enter and breaks away, patting his shoulder. Toni looks ready to drop, so he's more than happy to take a break.

"Hey, you up for a few rounds?" she asks.

"Yes. Give me a second to change."

The good thing about Rosa is she knows my body language. Not just because we were lovers, but because we've worked closely together in some harrowing circumstances. I trust her with my life in a fight.

We go head-to-head for a few hours until neither of us can lift our arms any longer, yet I'm still left with this strange energy in the pit of my stomach. My mind keeps wandering to the Moorsides upstairs. Have Phillip and Mark managed to convince Bonnie that Italy is the only safe option?

Walking to my room, I spare a glance at the door opposite me. I know Bonnie isn't there. Shaking my head, I shower and change. There are still a few more daylight hours, which means I need to work. Having taken care of the business side of things, I direct my energy towards Giani and Gisto. I need to know where they are and what they're doing. I'm sick and tired of being one step behind.

Picking up my phone, I call Luke. He's a young Australian who set up a bar in our local village five years ago. He's been on our payroll the entire time and keeps me in the loop regarding the Arellos.

"Hey, boss," he calls, "I thought you'd be back by now."

Me too.

"Soon. We're getting ready to head back in the next couple of days. How are things your end?" He knows I'm not asking for idle gossip. I want details on Giani.

"Quiet. He hasn't been to the bar in a few days, which is strange. He has to be running out of cigarettes by now. I've got a new shipment in the back waiting for him. I can't sell the nasty things to anyone else. He's the only one on the island who wants them!"

Damn, that *is* strange. Giani has claimed Luke's Bar as his local watering hole and spends at least two hours a day there, drinking. So why the disruption of his schedule? It's definitely odd he's not champing at the bit to collect his gold-lined cigarettes. The man smokes two packs a day.

"And Gisto?"

"Yeah, he's here now, actually. Got a shiner on his face. His dad's handiwork, I guess."

So, Giani is pissed. Nothing new there, I guess. But pairing Gisto's black eye with the fact Giani has skipped his time at the bar has my hackles up.

"Thanks, Luke. We'll talk soon." A gut feeling tells me we got to Bonnie just in time.

I sit, deliberating what to do next. Bonnie is safe here for the time being. We have enough family around to guard her. She doesn't need me babysitting. My time would be better spent figuring out what the Arellos are up to.

Jogging to Lorenzo's office, I knock before entering. He's standing by the window again looking...sad. He turns to briefly look at me before staring back out the window.

"I'm going back tonight," I announce.

That gets his attention. "What's happened?"

"Nothing as of yet, but something's stirring. I can feel it. I need to get back now. You can follow with Bonnie and her parents in a couple of days once I've made sure it's safe to return."

"But—"

"No buts, Lorenzo. It's happening. You need to snap out of whatever the hell this is," I say, waving my hand around the office. "Hiding away isn't helping."

"It's not that simple," he begins.

"I don't want to hear it," I snap. "I've got too much on my plate to worry about you right now."

Harsh, but true. This wilting sad sack is no use to me. I need Don Ferrante to step up and help me. Lorenzo has always reacted better to the truth, no matter how hard it is to say or hear.

He studies me for a second before pulling at his shirt sleeves. Once they are fixed, he does the same to his tie.

"You're right. And yes, I'm aware of how many times I've said that lately."

I grin. "I'll call you when I arrive."

"Be safe, Allegra."

"Always."

Taking a deep breath, I leave and head straight to my room to pack.

I'm going home.

11

Bonnie

I HAVEN'T HELD ONTO my parents like this since I was a child. All my bravado and anger simply went up in smoke the second I saw my dads. The past twenty-four hours catch up to me in one heart-stuttering moment, and all I can do is sob into their embrace.

"You're okay, pumpkin."

I'm not okay. Not in the slightest. Everything feels overwhelming. "I..."

"Deep breaths, sweetheart. We're here now," Pop says. Dad wraps his longer arms around me and Pop.

"Hey, I want some love," Kelley calls from the bed, which makes me laugh. We've spent the past few hours talking things through. She's almost convinced me it's a good idea to go along with Allegra's plan. I apologised again for snapping at her, and then we spent a good hour trying to get a comb through her hair.

"Come here, Kels," Pop laughs, breaking away from me and Dad to take Kelley gently in his arms. "How ya doing, kiddo?"

Kelley and I are both in our early thirties. We're not exactly kids, but Pop always calls us that.

"Sore, but okay. I'm ready to get out of this bed. It's my shoulder that hurts, not my legs" she huffs.

"Why don't we go for a walk? The gardens are lovely from what I can see," Dad says, looking out the window.

I shake my head. "We should stay here and talk. I'm so glad you're here. Maybe you can talk the crazy blonde lady into letting us go home."

It's childish calling Allegra that, but I need to put a firmer barrier between us. When she said my name after I'd threatened grievous bodily harm, my nervous system went haywire. I've never heard *Bonnie* sound so...dangerous before.

"Take a seat, sweetheart," Pop says, patting the spot next to him and Kelley.

A sinking feeling makes itself at home in my chest. I'd wondered if my dads knew about Lorenzo, and I think I'm about to get the answer.

Dad crouches by my knee. He smells of Gucci for Men, whereas Pop smells like Versace. I've always ribbed them for being cologne snobs. It's the only stylish thing about them. Pop has a wool obsession like me, and Dad wears garish bow ties most days.

"Can you just tell me?" I ask. "I've had enough surprises lately. I can't deal with any more secrets."

Pop squeezes my thigh, and Dad drops his head. "I'm sorry, pumpkin. We never thought this would happen. Lorenzo promised you weren't in any danger as long as your identity was protected."

My throat bobs as I try to swallow. "You've known about him all this time?"

Dad looks up into my eyes. "We've never met the man until today. We received a letter when we finalised your adoption."

"What did it say?"

Pop sighs. "Nothing and everything, I suppose. Lorenzo felt it necessary to warn us. The letter was brief and didn't give any details. He said that letter would be the last time we would ever hear from him, and at that moment, my dear, we were so delighted to finally have you, we chose to believe him and forget about it."

Dad takes Pop's hand. "Look, we're not stupid people, Bonnie. The letter alluded to a genuine threat to your life. It didn't exactly paint your biological father as a good person. It's not like he was a known criminal. Well, not in the UK, anyway. But the clues were there. Clearly, he was into things no child should ever be a part of. So we decided to leave it be. Neither your Pop nor I saw a benefit in digging into something that could bring you harm. And...as time went by, we didn't see the point in worrying you with it. Lorenzo was never supposed to reappear."

"Darling, if for one second we thought having Lorenzo in your life would've been beneficial, we would have told you," Pop adds on.

"Ignorance was the way to keep you safe," Dad finishes.

Does this change anything? Probably not. Whether they knew about him or not doesn't erase what's happening here and now. Do I wish they'd told me? I'm not sure. Maybe I would have felt curious and looked into Lorenzo Ferrante. I can understand why my dads wouldn't want me doing that.

"You're going to tell me to go to Sicily, aren't you?"

Pop strokes my hair like he did when I was a little girl and struggling to process the world. "What do you want to do?"

I look at him with raised eyebrows. "I want to go home and forget all about this. I want to go to work and then go home to my microwave meals."

That pulls furrowed brows from both parents. Okay, so Allegra's assessment of my life may have stung, because it was pretty much spot on, although the wool dig was unnecessary.

"Okay, now what do you think you should do?" Dad asks.

I blow a raspberry. "I should go to the stupid villa?"

Pop and Dad chuckle. "I think that's the right call, sweetheart," Pop soothes.

"You're both coming too, though. If the threat is as bad as Lorenzo thinks, I want you with me."

Pop nods. "Of course. We're due for a holiday, anyway."

"Should we call Pete?" Kelley asks. She's nibbling on her bottom lip. "I mean, if people are looking for you, we have to assume they know who your friends are."

My first reaction is to laugh. Allegra is going to lose her shit if I demand Pete be brought along, too. "Maybe I should ask Lorenzo. He knows who we're up against."

"I'll go," Dad says. My guess is he wants a few more words with him. "While I do that, why don't you help Kelley get washed and dressed? It's a beautiful day. No need to stay cooped up in here." His eyes are roaming over the wallpaper and furniture. His dislike is written all over his face.

Once Kelley is washed—and her hair tamed—we head outside. I'm on edge waiting for Toni the Giant to pop out and shout at me for leaving the house. He doesn't. Actually, he waves as I walk by. His hair is still greased back, and he's wearing the same dark suit as before, but for whatever reason, he looks less threatening in the daylight.

As soon as we step outside, the roar of the ocean pulls my attention. One side of the property looks over a sheer cliff face. The ocean is choppy, and waves batter the rocks. I am flabbergasted we made it to the cave entrance without being impaled.

Looking around doesn't give me any clue as to where we are. I guess it doesn't matter considering we'll be moving on soon. Kelley links her good arm with me as we stroll. Dark Land Rovers line the front of the mansion. Cliché, in my opinion. The Ferrante family could at least *pretend* this isn't a mob house.

"It's good to get some fresh air," Kelley says. My dads are still talking to Lorenzo, and as much as I want to know what's going on, Kelley needs me more.

"Kel, are you sure you want to come along? You could visit your mum or something. You don't need to put yourself in danger for me."

"I'm not in danger with you, though. That's the point, Bonnie."

I sneak a side glance. "What about Allegra? She shot you!"

Kelley takes a deep breath. "She did, and I can't lie; she's fucking terrifying, like way more than in books."

"She's an ass," I state.

"But she's still really hot, right?"

Before I can answer, Allegra steps out of the house, talking to a woman I've yet to meet. They are talking closely and quietly. Behind them, Toni exits with several suitcases. He throws them in the back of one of the ridiculously large Land Rovers. Allegra kisses the woman on the cheeks and climbs in the back of the car.

I watch the car back out and drive off. "Where's she going?" I bark.

Kelley eyes me again. I'm starting to think I've got something on my face. Why is everyone studying me every time I open my mouth?

"Allegra is travelling to Italy this evening," a voice says, way too close to my ear. I didn't notice the woman Allegra was speaking to walk over. Turning, I do my best to not cower. She has the same energy as Allegra and I'm sure she's just as deadly.

"Good for her."

Scary woman chuckles. "You don't fool me," she says quietly. "I see you."

"Um, okay. Sorry, do I know you?"

She shakes her head. "We've never met face to face."

"Right. Well, nice to meet you..."

"Rosa. And you are Bonnie Moorside, long-lost daughter of the big man."

I shake my head. "Biologically. That's it. Anyway, we're going to continue our walk. That is, if I'm still allowed that basic freedom."

Another wolfish grin. "I see what Allegra means. See you around, Sparky."

I don't love that nickname, but I think I've given enough snark for one day.

"What was that about?" Kelley asks. I shrug. "She was scary, too."

"Oh, Kel. They are all scary. Remember who they are."

"Hey, I said I was drugged up when I was talking shite about Beth."

"Uh-huh. You're forgetting I was there earlier when she changed your dressing."

She laughs. "I can look."

"Sure. As long as you remember what these people do."

She bops her head. "Yeah, okay. I'll give you the same advice then, Bonnie."

My head whips around. "Excuse me?"

"Oh, please! I see your lustful stares at Allegra."

"She's a nut job, Kelley. What you're seeing is disdain."

"Thin line between—"

"Do not finish that sentence. Now, do you want to stretch your legs or not?"

"Defensive," she murmurs.

Our bickering is interrupted by my dads. "Hey, kiddos. Nice out here, isn't it?"

"Better than the view from down there," I say, pointing towards the ocean.

"Ah, you got the boat tour too, huh," Dad says. That would have gone down like a ton of bricks because he gets violently seasick.

"We did. I'm hoping we can go out the front way when we leave."

"Speaking of which," Pop says. "Lorenzo wants us on a plane in the morning. Allegra has already left, and I don't think he feels comfortable being here without her."

"Because she's a violent killer and he needs her to do the dirty work?" I spit.

My dads' eyes go wide, and they share a look; one I've witnessed hundreds of times before, especially in my teenage years when I was particularly moody. "That's a lot of anger, pumpkin."

"Maybe I've got a lot to be angry about," I snap. Blimey, what's got into me?

"You have. That's true. So let's talk about it, sweet-heart."

"No, I'm tired of talking. I'm sorry, I'll be fine. Maybe I need some time alone. I'll see you later." And then I walk off back to the house, back to the room I couldn't wait to be away from, and yet it now feels like the only place I can think clearly.

I have to get a grip on myself. My parents are here and we're all safe. That's all that matters. Everything else is just background noise. Allegra leaving without a word shouldn't matter. But it does.

I've only been in the room for a few minutes before I'm feeling agitated. Storming out, I set off down the stairs with no particular destination. Poking my head around several doors, I come to a screeching halt when I enter what can only be described as the most beautiful room I have ever seen. Yes, there is still dark wood everywhere, but that can be forgiven because the wood is housing thousands upon thousands of books. I have never seen a private library this large before.

It's times like this I totally understand Belle staying with the Beast. Books are a game changer. Sod true love; give me a bunch of novels any day of the week. My brain breathes a sigh of relief, and I know what I need to do to work off this bad mood. I need to organise. I can already see the shelves are in no order whatsoever. That's about to change.

I don't hear the door open. I'm surrounded by books on the floor, and I've never been happier. So far, it's less organised than when I started, but I can't be blamed for getting distracted. Two legs step into my line of sight. Expensive-looking Italian loafers shuffle nervously. Placing down the book I've been salivating over, I look up to see Lorenzo staring at me with wonder in his eyes.

"You're so much like your mother," he says. "She loved this room, too."

Standing, I look around. "Sorry about the mess. I'll tidy it up, I promise. I just needed something to take my mind off…"

He smiles at me softly and I see myself in him again. It's really weird if I'm honest.

"Take your time and do whatever you need to do. I hope before all this is over, you'll give me a chance to talk to you. About your mother…or about myself. Whatever you'd like to know."

"Maybe. I… I'm sorry. I know you want more than that, but I'm struggling with who you are, if truth be told."

He bobs his head. "Understandable. Just keep an open mind. That's all I ask."

I watch him leave and feel myself crumple until I'm back on the floor. I wish there was a "My Dad is a Mobster" manual. I could do with some guidance. My mind drifts to

Allegra, and I wonder what it was like for her growing up with Lorenzo.

I wonder what kind of woman she would have been outside of this life.

12

Allegra

STANDING ON THE BALCONY, I inhale the sweet smell of home. It's dark, but that's fine. I don't need to see the land to feel at peace. The insects singing and the smell of the vines are enough for now. Tomorrow, I will take a long walk around the property and recentre myself.

I thought coming home would solve everything until I realised my problems were coming with me. By problems, I mean Bonnie Moorside. She's going to be underfoot for God knows how long. As much as I'd love to lose myself in the vines for the next few weeks, I can't. My days will be spent shackled to my desk, trying to untangle Lorenzo's mess. Bonnie will be a constant presence I could do without.

On the plane ride home, I had to have an uncomfortable conversation with myself. Actually, it was more of an uncomfortable realisation. Bonnie gets under my skin and derails my usually impenetrable Ice Bitch persona. She rattles me, and there has only ever been one other person to have done that: Petra.

Petra Cortez was my first love and my rival for years. She was whip-smart and full of fire, just like Bonnie. We would never have survived, though. I know that now. But at the time, I thought we could overcome all our obstacles. The main one being we were parts of two different families that hardly ever saw eye to eye.

Our relationship lasted three years. Most of the time we had to sneak around, which in the beginning was fun, however I learned in the end, Petra had played me for a fool. She used the fact she could unbalance me to her advantage. After stealing valuable intel from my office, she left without a word. I'd been used.

For a long time, my stupid heart couldn't let go of the idea Petra had to have loved me. How could she have faked the passion? I refused to believe it was all a lie. That was until I saw her eighteen months later with her husband. We were at a gala, and the moment she spotted me, her eyes went wide and her face paled.

By that time, I had hardened myself even more. She thought I was cold back then. Petra had no idea what I'd become since she humiliated me and broke my heart. I'd thrown myself into work after she ghosted me. I made new contacts and set about plotting my revenge. It was Lorenzo who'd picked me up and dusted me off. He told me to stop wallowing and take back control. So that's what I did.

Over the course of those eighteen months, I systematically bought all of Petra's and her husband's debts. He was a terrible gambler, which I suspect was part of the reason she went through the whole charade of loving me to steal information that would make him some money. I'm sure it paid off in the short term, but his addiction was beyond her control, and within a year he had debt up to his greasy hair again.

So, once I procured the debt, I also began buying large amounts of stock in Petra's family businesses. By the time I saw her at the gala, I owned her. She just didn't know it. People may claim I never really loved her if I was able to be so callous in the end.

Wrong. I loved Petra with all my heart, but I would not be a victim. All this "turn the other cheek" and "be the bigger person" bullshit is for the weak. Someone scorns me, I return it tenfold. Life threw tragedy and pain at me from a young age. Well, I gave life the middle finger. And I gave Petra twenty-four hours to pay her debts and vacate her house. Petra's family name was burned from the history books. I solidified the Ferrante family as the most powerful name in Italy that night.

My trip down memory lane is a warning to myself. Bonnie affects me like Petra did. Looks-wise, they are day and night. But their personalities are far too similar for comfort. I'll never let myself be made a fool again, which is why I need to keep Bonnie away from me. And therein lies the problem. She will be here twenty-four seven. The villa is big, but it's still a small world, as they say.

I can't even travel for work, considering Lorenzo has put me in charge of her safety. Hopefully, having her dads, best friend, and apparently other best friend, Pete, here will distract her enough we can avoid each other.

That's a tomorrow problem, though. Right now, I just want to bask in the fact I am home alone, with a gorgeous, full-bodied red, under the spectacular Sicilian sky. No matter my worries, a few hours sitting here cures all ailments.

Of course, the universe has other plans. Apparently, I wronged the gods somewhere along the line.

"Excuse me, Allegra," Enzo, head of security at the villa, says, "we have a problem."

Sighing, I turn and slip back into boss mode. "What's wrong?"

"Another shipment has been attacked."

"Did you catch them?"

He nods. "I thought you'd like a chat with them."

My eyebrow raises. I don't usually get my hands dirty nowadays. The family deals with troublemakers, so for Enzo to include me, means whoever he caught is no lackey.

"Lead the way."

Enzo takes me to the cellar. It's cliché, but they are useful for this type of activity for a reason. No windows, half-metre thick walls, and no interruptions.

As I step onto the cellar floor, I almost falter in my step. "Gisto. This is a surprise."

Why is Gisto directly involved in hijacking our shipments? He's far too important to be doing such a job, especially when the risk of being caught is so high. It doesn't make sense.

"Allegra." His eye is bruised, but it's a few days old. Presumably, it's the work of his father, like Luke mentioned. Apart from that, he is unharmed. The family knows better than to beat the son of Giani Arello.

I drag over a chair and place it opposite Gisto. He isn't tied up, but two of my biggest men stand at either side of his shoulders.

"Fancied yourself a little fun this evening, it seems."

He shrugs. Sitting back, I cross one leg over the other and regard him silently. There is a game at play, and I need to figure out what the rules are. Gisto wouldn't have attacked a shipment without his father's say-so. Giani wanted him to be caught, but why? And then it dawns on me. I can't help but chuckle, which earns a confused look from Gisto.

"You're free to go home, Gisto. Would you like a ride?"

He looks utterly confused. Giani's plan was rudimentary at best, but could have been effective if it were anyone but me he was dealing with. As I mentioned before, Giani still plays by the old rules. He still uses the old-school Mafiosi handbook. Unfortunately for him, I do not.

Giani expected me to teach Gisto a lesson. He probably thought I'd be so consumed with rage because Gisto had so brazenly tried to steal from me, my ego would have taken over and I would hurt Gisto. If I did fall into the trap, Giani would have declared a vengeance war. One family *openly* hurting another paves the way for a legitimate fight for honour and all that macho bullshit. Ridiculous, if you ask me. It's not the 1920s, for heaven's sake.

Frankly, I'm more offended Giani thought I'd fall for such a poorly thought-out plan. He must be getting desperate. The Arello family has been hitting our imports for a while now, without any backlash from us. Giani is clearly getting tired and wants to push me.

"Enzo, please make sure Gisto gets home safely. Oh, and give him a bottle of our house wine. For the wife," I say with a smile. Poor Gisto; his father is not going to be pleased and I'm sure he'll get the brunt of his outburst.

With that taken care of, I bid Enzo and the rest of the family good night. It's been a long day, and by the looks of things, the coming days are going to be hell. Sending a quick update to Lorenzo, I shut myself in my ensuite, run the bath, and sink into the bubbles.

As easy as it was to figure out Giani's plan, I have to be mindful. A desperate man does desperate things. If he finds out Bonnie is here, I have no doubt he will try something stupid. It's unlikely he will be obvious about it. I can't envisage him storming the villa and mowing us down, not with other families close by. We might be rivals, but overall, we look out for each other to preserve our way of life. If Giani breaks the rules, the Ferrante family will be the least of his worries.

So, I need to be cautious. Bonnie must stay within the perimeter of the villa and inner gardens. The risk of her having an "accident" whilst in the vineyard is too great, especially as the vineyard is the biggest on the island.

Great, I can't wait to have that discussion with her. No, not a discussion. What am I thinking? She's not my equal here. I'm in charge of her safety and she'll do as she's told.

You're fooling yourself, Allegra.

Sinking below the water, I let out a scream that burns my lungs. I suddenly feel bone-tired—not from the travel, but from the weight of shit I have to deal with. I've focused solely on making Lorenzo and the Ferrante family proud. But sometimes I forget the cost of the job.

The brief respite I had earlier is well and truly gone now. No amount of stargazing will help. I just need to sleep. As I towel off and slip under silk sheets, my phone lights up. I want to hurl the thing across the room. Gritting my teeth, I open the message to see what barrage of shit I have to deal with now. The message is from Rosa.

Rosa 11:27 p.m.

You're in trouble this time, Allegra.
She's going to eat you alive!

I regret opening my mouth. Last night, I may have vented to Rosa about our new houseguest.

Allegra 11:29 p.m.

Stay in your lane, Rosa.

Rosa 11:30 p.m.

You don't scare me, Al. I can't wait to
see this blow up in your face!

Of course, Rosa was there through the Petra debacle, so she'd immediately latched on to my irritation with Bonnie as being something more than one person detesting the other. She was insufferable last night. I couldn't exactly deny it, though. My feelings for Bonnie are confusing, but only because she reminds me of Petra—not because I have any *genuine* emotions about her.

Rosa found the entire thing hilarious. She gets off on watching me squirm. This time, though, she will be disap-

126

pointed. Bonnie hates me as much as I dislike her. We just have to get through this threat unscathed and everything will go back to normal.

Normal. What does that even mean? I'm more worried I don't know the answer to that, than anything else. I thought claiming the title of Donna Malgeri was everything I wanted, but once in a while, a sliver of doubt creeps in. Having to be icy all the time is draining. I feel most of my life is spent playing politics with other families, and I'm starting to question why I bother. Unbeknownst to the other families and somewhat to Lorenzo, I have taken the Ferrante family business on a more aboveboard route.

We make more money with legitimate businesses than we do our underground ones. I've not suddenly grown a conscience; it just makes sense. The law is cracking down harder and harder on our enterprises, and I, for one, will never see the inside of a prison. The days of disappearing people to deal with any unwanted attention are gone. As much as I enjoyed taking my frustration out on other bad guys, it is not feasible anymore. We have to be smarter, and the way to do that is to go legit.

Still, we do have a few practices that are frowned upon, but those just hurt the rich. No harm, no foul in my book. Our world sees me as a bloodthirsty animal; an image

I have encouraged. Being a woman in this line of work is no joke. Better that they fear me. But it's been a while since I've used violence to my advantage. The incident with Kelley, notwithstanding. Maybe I am finally growing a conscience if I'd rather hit the obnoxiously rich where it hurts than physically hurt innocent civilians. Huh, that's something to ruminate on.

Putting the phone on silent, I lay back and stare at the ceiling. Sometimes I feel like I have two personalities: One that still needs to prove my worth to Lorenzo and the family, and the other that is tired and wants to stop.

I am Allegra Malgeri, and I am...tired.

13

Bonnie

IF I WERE WRITING a book, I'd name this chapter "Pete". Because the second I see him step out of the car, I know he's about to stand centre stage. And I'm okay with that. Far too much focus has been on me lately and I'm ready for a break.

We're heading to the airport soon, but I refused to leave until Pete arrived. I've got Kelley, who makes up one half of my friend support system. She's like me: introverted and a massive geek. She is my logic. Pete makes up the second half. He's outgoing, spontaneous, and extroverted. He's not afraid to challenge my reserved personality and sometimes I need that—like in a situation where you've been kidnapped by mobsters. If anyone can help me get through this, it's Pete, with Kelley reining him in when needed.

"Well, fuck me, honey. I know I told you to get a life, but I didn't quite mean this," he says, waving flamboyantly at the giant house. "Love the look, by the way," he finishes, grabbing my shoulders and looking me up and down.

"Not my choice," I reply, tugging him into a hug.

"Which part?"

"All of it. I'm sorry you've been dragged into it, P."

He sucks his teeth. "Fuck that. This is excellent. I would have been super pissed if you'd left me out. Hey, what happened to you, Frizz?"

Kelley jabs him with her good arm. "I got shot, you arse!"

Pete clutches his imaginary pearls. "My, my, it's all happening here, isn't it? So, when are we leaving?"

Rubbing my forehead, I let out an exasperated chuckle. "Aren't you going to ask what all this is about? I'm pretty sure you've just been forcefully removed from wherever you were, and you're not even bothered."

Dropping the pearls, he flicks his imaginary long hair. "Some big, gorgeous bloke turns up at work telling me I'd won a trip, and I had to leave with him immediately, no questions asked. Fuck, colour me intrigued."

"How have you not been murdered yet?" Kelley asks, and I wholeheartedly agree.

"Whatever. So, when and where are we going? Oh, hey, your dads are here too. Oh, wow, who is that silver fox?"

Pete is like a child after ten Red Bulls sometimes.

"That's Lorenzo Ferrante," I say quietly. Lorenzo is talking to my dads again. They shake hands and Lorenzo slips into the back of his car. Pop turns and ushers us over.

"Hey, Pete, good to see you, kiddo."

"Hi, Mark. Looking good. I like that cardigan."

"Thanks, it's new. Anyway, are you all ready to go?"

"Ready and raring. Let's get this show on the road, darlings."

I notice Toni's eyebrows lift. I doubt he's come across someone like Pete before.

Pete, Kelley, and I take one car, with my parents following behind. It would feel like we're celebrities if the people chauffeuring us weren't carrying pistols.

"So, who is Lorenzo, and how can I get a meeting with him?"

I grimace automatically. "Eww, no, Pete. He's off limits, okay?"

"Why? What am I missing?"

"He's Bonnie's bio dad," Kelley says, shifting in her seat to get more comfortable. "He's a major mobster baddie."

"Fuck off," Pete laughs. He stops when we don't share his enthusiasm. "You're being serious?"

"Yes, Pete, dead serious. Trust me, I know how it sounds. I thought *you'd* hired the woman who took me, as part of a joke at first."

"I wish," he laughs. "That would have been epic."

"Sure, a real fun time," I deadpan. "Anyway, my mistake got Kelley shot, and I quickly understood we were in real danger."

Kelley rubs her shoulder before piping in. "Until we arrived at the house. Lorenzo explained everything to Bonnie. Allegra, that's the scary woman who has a penchant for violence against innocent bookworms, didn't know who she was, and I don't think she was supposed to scare either of us to death. Or, you know, shoot me."

"Where's this Allegra, then? Is she hot?"

"Keep it in your boxers, buddy," I growl. "She's awful. Like the worst. Ice queen on steroids, and with a firearm."

"So, she's smokin', right?" Pete says, wiggling his eyebrows.

"Oh, yeah, super-hot," Kelley answers, "and she left for Italy yesterday. You'll meet her soon. Or if you're lucky, not at all."

"Italy, where? Rome? Florence?"

"Sicily," Toni gruffs from the driver's seat.

"Well thanks, handsome," Pete replies. He flirts with everyone, I swear; however, I didn't expect Toni to blush. Interesting.

"According to Allegra, the villa we will be staying at is super secure."

"Right, yeah. So, I get you're related to a mob boss...but why are you and the fam being shipped off to a secure location?"

I spend the rest of the journey to the private airport explaining everything that has come to light so far. If Toni weren't in earshot, I'd ask Pete and Kelley to give me some advice regarding Lorenzo and his wish to speak with me. I'm still on the fence about it.

"And how are you feeling about all this, Bon?" Pete is the only one who gets away with calling me that. Although, he's the reason Janice started calling me Bon Bon, so maybe I should rescind the permission.

"Overwhelmed. How else would I feel?"

"Uh, I don't know...pumped? This is exactly what you need, my friend!"

"Did you hear any of the story I just told you, Pete?"

"Hell yeah, I did. And from what I can see, you might as well milk it for everything it's worth. You're going to a beautiful country, and staying at what I guess will be a luxurious villa. Food, drink, and hot people. It's a gift from the gods."

"But—"

"No buts, Bonnie. Look, you're going to be safe. Let the tough guys sort out the shit. You, Kelley, and I can just lay back and enjoy a holiday. You need it, Bonnie. I know I joke about your sad life."

"Harsh."

"True. I joke, but part of me worries...about you both," he says, glaring at Kelley, too. "There's a quiet life, and then there is acting like an octogenarian at thirty. You feel me?"

"I do not," I protest, but Pete cackles like a witch.

"Yes, you do. By all means, do the whole reading thing, but maybe try to balance it with actually experiencing life. That's all I'm saying."

"We're here," Toni grumbles.

"He's a big bear of a man I'd like to climb," Pete murmurs, licking his lips. Snapping his attention back to Kelley and me, he smiles. "You're about to board a private jet," he says, pointing out the window where a very expensive-looking plane stands waiting for us. "Life is passing you by, ladies. Time to grab it by the tits and ride it out."

"That is a horrible turn of phrase," Kelley replies, "but I get it."

"Bonnie?" Pete asks.

Two sets of eyes bore into me.

"Fine. It's going to be a holiday. There—happy?"

Pete claps excitedly. "Fucking ecstatic. Let's roll."

None of my worries have gone away, but having agreed to treat this less like a kidnapping and hostage situation, and more of a holiday away with friends, I have to say I'm feeling better. The complimentary Cristal doesn't hurt either.

Pop and Dad are sitting up front with Lorenzo. I guess they're trying to give us "youngsters" some space. My parents are pretty good at reading my needs. After yesterday's little temper tantrum, they've given me a wide berth. It's how they helped me get through puberty.

Before I know it, we've taken off and landed, and I'm positively tipsy. Kelley is looking a little glassy-eyed too.

We're such lightweights. It's only when Kelley and I start singing, that Pete hands out water bottles.

We disembark and ungracefully fall into the back of another blacked-out Land Rover. Toni doesn't look so happy with being our driver again, especially when Kelley starts singing.

I don't usually drink that much, and even when I do have a tipple, I know my limits. Unlike now, as I'm well and truly over my two-drink limit, but I'm also well beyond caring.

"Toni, you delicious specimen of a man, do you have any music?" Pete calls. Without saying a word, Toni turns up the radio. I'm guessing he wants to drown us out.

We sing and boogie in the backseat with water and more booze Pete pilfered from the plane. It's Kelley's gasp that stops us from warbling. I practically climb over my friends to see what the hullabaloo is about.

We're driving up to the most beautiful building I think I've ever seen. Fields of vines surround us, and the view of the ocean is incredible. If there's a pool, I might just die. It's a dream come true.

And then I see her: the dark angel that ruins my newfound happiness. Allegra stands on a balcony, looking down on us. I can't see her eyes, but I know they will be trying to drill a hole into the car.

"Who is *that*?" Pete whispers.

"Allegra," I reply, a little breathier than I'd like. Clearing my throat, I sit back in my seat. "Stay out of her way, Pete. She's bad news."

The cars pull up outside the old-looking wooden doors. I wonder if they are the originals. I'm guessing the villa is longstanding. It has a kind of charm to it that makes me think it's seen a lot through its time. Maybe that's the romance reader in me trying to put a positive spin on the situation.

Embarrassingly, I fall out the side of the car and land at the feet of Rosa, who chuckles, "Allegra is waiting to see you."

"Oh, how wonderful," I sneer.

God, can't I just have a day, or even a few hours, to settle in? Maybe just clean myself up from the drunk mess I seem to be right now. The last thing I want is to give the horrid woman any more ammo. I'm sure she'll revel in mocking me.

Ignoring everyone, I stumble behind Rosa into the villa. It's as gorgeous inside as it is out, but I don't have any time to stop and take it in. Rosa is on a mission. She stops us outside a dark wooden door. Two sharp knocks and then she opens the door, pushing me through it. I whirl around, ready to give her a piece of my mind, but she's already gone.

"Welcome to Sicily, Bonnie."

Blimey, that voice. It's so wrong I find it attractive.

"I said I'd come if my parents agreed, didn't I?"

I'm not expecting the tired sigh she lets out, or the dark circles under her eyes.

"You did, and I appreciate you keeping your word. I apologise for taking up your time. I know you've probably had a long day travelling. I presume Pete arrived without incident?"

She seems...different—resigned—and I don't like it.

"He did. Thank you for agreeing to take him in as well."

She bows her head slightly. "I'll skip straight to it. You dislike me, and that's fine, but you are in my home now, and I hope you will treat it, and me, with respect. I'll leave you alone unless there is an issue, so please go where you like inside, however, I need you to venture no further than the interior garden when outside. I don't ask this of you lightly. Our land is vast and too big to fully secure for you to go out any further, alone. The security personnel have specific jobs they must maintain, so I need to trust you'll not do anything to put yourself or anyone else in danger."

I don't like it, and I naturally want to do the opposite. I won't, though. As much as I hate all of this, Allegra and Lorenzo have promised to keep us safe, and they've brought Pete here without question.

"I'll do as you ask."

"Appreciated. Now, please go and enjoy the house. The pool is out back, and the chef knows to give you anything you want."

I stand there for a second, not knowing what to say. This is the most normal interaction we've had since meeting.

"Thanks," I manage. I suddenly need another drink.

14

Allegra

MY PLAN TO STAY out of the way has so far been successful. Bonnie, Kelley, and this Pete fellow—who I have yet to introduce myself to—have spent their time here so far, drinking our cellars dry and lounging by the pool. I honestly didn't think Ms Moorside had it in her. She's a far cry from the wool-clad nerd we picked up last week.

Another surprise is her lack of attitude toward the fact I confiscated her hideous clothing. It's not something I would usually trouble myself with. After all, why should I care how the woman dresses? I'll admit, that once I saw her in a pencil skirt and blouse, I knew I couldn't let her hide away a moment longer. Bonnie had a body to worship, and in all truth, I wanted to get a rise out of her. I've enjoyed fucking with her; what can I say?

The second she arrived with her bag, I had it removed and replaced by a full wardrobe of the finest Italian clothes. The morning after their arrival, I waited patiently for her to storm into my office, ranting and raving, demanding I return her sack of wool. She didn't. And I was wholly disappointed.

Bonnie hasn't so much as looked at me since our short meeting in my office, and it's thrown me for somewhat of a loop. But then I remind myself this is exactly what I wanted. I'd promised I'd keep my distance and focus on work, even though each day feels more of a grind than the next.

Everything has been quiet on the Arello front, and as unnerving as that is, I can't afford to waste time waiting for Giani's next move. I've doubled security around the villa and paid off a few more dock employees to keep an eye out for anything untoward. I'm yet to figure out how I'm going to get the Arellos to back off without bloodshed.

Lorenzo wasn't impressed that Gisto tried to mess with another shipment, and it took a bit of time to calm him down. But this is why I'm in charge. Lorenzo is tired, and his patience for these types of games is well and truly depleted. I'm not far behind in that regard. If I'd not been here to smooth things over, I'm sure Lorenzo's temper would have played right into Giani's hands and we'd be in the middle of a war right now.

Thankfully, I contained the situation and encouraged Lorenzo to concentrate on Bonnie and her dads. The man wants to get to know his daughter, and I'd rather he attempt that than get in my way. So far, he's spent his time talking with Mark and Phillip. I wonder if they've been counselling him. It's strange they are so calm about everything, if you ask me.

My focus now, is on the vineyard. I have crates of wine to ship out and temporary pickers to hire. Plus, the "other" business will need attention soon. I hate having to go to the dockyards, but I don't trust anyone else to verify our cargo. I'm the one with an art degree, after all. Well, I have more than that. In a different life, I would have been an artist full-time, I think. But that's not the case and there's no point looking back. My skills are used to help verify, and sometimes recreate. Although it's been a few years since I've had to make a forgery.

Unlike our house guests, I have not been sunning myself and replacing my blood content with wine. A part of me is concerned about Bonnie. I may have stayed out of the way, but that hasn't stopped me from observing, and I think her behaviour is probably a little too out of character.

She's a relative stranger to me, but something tells me all this partying is going to end in tears.

Pete is the leader of their little group. I can tell his lifestyle is very different from Kelley's and Bonnie's. He's the instigator. I've heard him encouraging Bonnie to "let go". One time I heard him explain alcohol was invented for dealing with stress. I didn't like it.

I know it's my fault Bonnie is feeling like this. How I handled her, and the days following, was unprofessional. And I probably made the situation far more stressful than it needed to be. I still blame Lorenzo for that, though.

Being back here in my sanctuary has allowed me to process my behaviour. I let my anger towards Lorenzo cloud my actions. I behaved how other families would have, and that's not okay. But it doesn't matter now; Bonnie and her friends will only ever see me as a ruthless criminal, which I probably deserve. If only Bonnie understood how complicated the situation is.

There I go again! It makes no sense that I even *want* Bonnie to understand. We've interacted a handful of times and they've all been terrible. Yet no matter how much I scold and remind myself of the similarities between Petra and Bonnie, I can't help but gravitate toward her, even if it is just a quick glance out the window to see what she's doing.

The day I took Bonnie Moorside irrevocably changed my life, and I don't know why! It's like my universe shifted the second we clashed. I just can't get back into my usual flow. All the voices in my head that were becoming despondent to the monotony of fighting for power, have only got louder. I can't tuck them away as easily anymore. The only light in my day is working in the vineyard.

I've taken to wandering the fields when the office becomes too stifling. Rosa has taken over the majority of managing the staff and security, allowing me a modicum of space to breathe.

I keep thinking everything will be fine when Bonnie and her family leave. At least I won't have to listen to any more pop music. But will it? Can I get the motivation back to keep dealing with family politics? Do I want to? I feel like I don't know myself anymore.

Until I met Bonnie, I revelled in the power I'd earned. I was able to push the unsavoury things I'd had to do to get where I am, to the back of my mind. But in such a short amount of time, the ruthless Allegra that set off to pick up some random woman on Lorenzo's behalf, is slowly slipping away, being replaced by someone I don't know.

It's almost nine in the evening now and the sun is starting to set. I'll never get used to the breathtaking views over the sea. The sun casts vibrant oranges and pinks across the sky. It's stunning.

I've been walking for a good half an hour, so I'm way out of the villa's secure perimeter. I'm not worried, though. I have my pistol, and even Giani Arello isn't stupid enough to come for me personally. Not because he's worried about what Lorenzo will do, but because he knows I will fuck up anyone who attempts to hurt me, and then I *would* be out for blood. The only reason I'm not now, is because Giani's attempts at hurting the family have been weak so far. Nothing he's done has warranted me to go into full Donna Malgeri mode.

A rustling two rows away has me on guard. It's probably a critter, but I'm naturally suspicious and guarded, so I reach for my gun. What I find both amuses me and infuriates me. Lying tangled in the grapes is a very inebriated Bonnie.

I've not seen her this afternoon, and now I know why. Rosa is going to get the full force of my anger when we get back. Bonnie will get it when she's sober, which by the state of her, will be tomorrow afternoon at some point.

"Bonnie? What are you doing out here?" My voice is sharp and makes her jump. Her eyes are bleary and red-rimmed. She's totally wasted.

"Look whotiz! Misssss Mafia Queen herself: Allegra-I'll-Shoot-Ya-Best-Friend-Ferrante."

I don't bother correcting her. I've been called worse. Never Mafia Queen, though. And I am a Ferrante in every way but blood.

"Bonnie, you're too far away from the villa."

"Pfft. I wanted a walk, so sue me. Or kidnap me and shoot me. I don't care. You won't get me, queeny. I know what your game is."

I'm totally lost. She's rambling, and I don't have time to decipher what the fucking hell she's talking about.

"Get up," I bark.

"No! You're not the boss of me. I won't marry you!"

Um...

"And you can stop looking at me with your eyes. They won't work either! Do you hear me, Sexy Allegra? Nothing will work. I won't be your sex slave!"

I'm definitely missing some context here.

"Just get up," I say, hooking my hands under her armpits. She's dead weight.

"No. I want to look at the sea. It's so pretty."

She's a stubborn toddler, I swear it!

"*Basta*!" I growl, but she doesn't stop. She sinks lower to the ground, making it impossible to pick her up. "Bonnie, get up!"

She sticks her tongue out. "No! I'm watching the pretty colours."

Dropping her arms, I stand and stretch my back. What the hell am I going to do? Looking around, I can't see any of our security, which isn't surprising considering how far out we are.

"Fine. If we watch the sunset, will you stand up after and let me take you back to the villa?"

She squints at me for a second and I think it's partly her thinking face and partly trying to get her eyes to focus. "Deal," she shouts, thrusting her hand out. "Shake on it, then, Sexy Allegra."

Now I do laugh. "Deal," I reply, giving her hand a solid shake. "Do you want to stand now, though, to see the horizon better? I can't imagine it's a great view from the dirt."

Another moment of contemplation before she gives a decisive nod and does her best to stand up. I catch her around the waist before she takes out my prize-winning plants.

"Stupid shoes," she grumbles until she looks down, confused. "Where are my stupid shoes?"

"No idea."

"Huh."

She allows me to guide her a little closer to the cliff's edge. The view really is breathtaking from up here.

"Please don't throw me off," she says and then burps.

"I have no intentions of that. I won't hurt you, Bonnie." I really want the words to stick.

"But you hurt Kelley. She's my bestie from another westie... No, that's not right. Sister from another mother. No, hang on..."

I roll my lips in to stop a laugh bubbling up. "Sister from another mister, I think is the correct phrase."

"Yes, that!" she declares, pointing her finger to the sky in triumph. Her eyes dart from the sunset to my eyes. She's waiting for me to say something.

"I've apologised for that. I know it was wrong." Jesus, it's like talking to a child.

Another squint of her eyes. "But you have a gun. You're a baddie and I don't like it. You're too pretty to be a baddie."

"I..." ...do *not* like her calling me a baddie. But I shouldn't be surprised. It all seems so black and white to people. Clearing my throat, I nod to the sun, which is almost gone. "You're missing it."

She looks at me for a second longer and then turns towards the sea. Her balance is atrocious, so I keep my arm around her waist. I feel her move into me a little more and my traitorous heart does a little dance.

Thankfully, she doesn't protest when I encourage her to walk with me. About fifteen minutes in and she's sagging against me, her eyes drooping.

Great.

Scooping her up, I hold her firmly in my arms. She doesn't protest, which leads me to believe she's already asleep. At least this way I can pick up the pace. I'm a sweaty mess by the time we arrive at the villa. Rosa is standing there, her face pale.

"Allegra, I—"

"Save it," I growl. Pushing through the door, I don't stop when Pete and Kelley come rushing over. I barge through them all and take Bonnie straight to her room. Laying her down on the unmade bed, I cover her with a light sheet. It's far too hot for anything more, and I'm not going to undress her. She's out like a light and drooling.

Softly closing the door behind me, fatigue suddenly hits me with force. I should go down and rip into Rosa, or into Bonnie's so-called friends, for letting her get into that state and allowing her to wander off.

I do neither of those things. I go to my room, shower, and slip under the covers. Instead of frustration, I start to laugh. Once I start, I can't stop. Bonnie's slurred words play in a loop. Forgetting about the whole "you're a baddie" thing, I concentrate on her calling me *Sexy Allegra*.

I'm going to have fun with that.

15

Bonnie

I'M DYING. ALL THE moisture in my body is gone and my skull feels like it's vacuum-packed my brain. This isn't the first day since being here I've woken up with a hangover, but it's the worst by far.

I can't even remember getting to bed. In fact, a whole chunk of yesterday is gone. The last thing I remember was Pete pouring me a mimosa at brunch. One turned into many and then...nothing. If yesterday followed the pattern we've got ourselves into recently, the three of us would have stayed around the pool, drinking and listening to music. But if we did that, why are my feet muddy? And why do I have it on my arse as well? Dammit, I really liked this skirt.

A sharp pain makes me moan out loud. I think it's my liver protesting. It's never had to deal with this amount of alcohol in all its existence. I need a bucket of water. But first... Yep, I need to vomit. Oh, God.

Now I've purged myself of a week's worth of alcohol, maybe I can try to get some water and food in me. Just the thought of eating turns my stomach more. I'm close to summoning the energy to go downstairs when my door flies open and Kelley spills in, looking worse for wear.

"Oh, thank God. I was so worried about you," she gasps. Flinging herself at me, I endure the bone-breaking hug until the stench of alcohol that still clings to her skin makes me gag.

"Kelley, you need to shower." She's not the only one. It feels like alcohol is leaking from every pore in my body.

She's nodding enthusiastically. "I know, and I will. I just had to make sure you were okay. I can't believe you wandered off. I was so scared."

"Do you remember what happened? Because I'm drawing a blank."

"Oh, God, I understand. I've only just started piecing things together again. It was the replay of Allegra barging past us with you in her arms that did it. I'm not likely to forget that in a hurry. She looked like she wanted to kill someone."

My jaw goes slack. "What did you say? Allegra had me..."

"In her arms. You were zonked. All muddy and dishevelled. We tried to come over to you but she near on ran us down. I think Pete fell in a giant plant pot. Oh, boy, she was pissed."

Allegra. Had me. In her arms? Fuck fuckity fuck.

"Crap." I try to run my hands through my hair, but my fingers snag on something. As gently as possible, I pluck what looks to be a bit of a plant. Yeah, I definitely did something stupid last night, and I'm guessing Allegra is going to be super mad. Damn it. I've done so well staying away from her.

Saying that, it's been a weird few days. I stayed out of sight but missed seeing her, which makes zero sense considering she's the Devil. I've also come to realise that I've possibly been letting go a little too much. I'm self-aware enough to know this is less "enjoying a holiday with friends" and more "drinking to cope". It's a shock my parents haven't intervened. Maybe they're doing it too.

Looking around the room, I take in the state of it. Clothes are strewn everywhere. I got super mad when I realised all *my* clothes were gone, only to find expensive replacements in the wardrobe. I was all geared up to storm into Allegra's office and have it out with her, but then I changed my mind. I didn't want to play her games, so I did a fashion show instead and embraced the situation.

If Allegra carried me to bed last night, she would have seen the mess I'd left. It must've looked like I've thrown a fit and trashed the place. I didn't. I just started to party and never got round to tidying up, which is so far from who I am, it's scary. I'm not handling this as well as I thought, apparently.

"Where's Pete?"

"By the pool. He's already on his second cocktail."

Ugh, the thought of alcohol is not helping. I cannot imbibe today.

"Ah, you're awake," Rosa says from my doorway, "and you look like shit. Good, you deserve it. Allegra wants to see you. Now!"

"C-can I have a shower first? I stink."

"No. I've just had my arse handed to me because of the stunt you pulled. Get your backside down there and don't make me ask you again." Rosa practically growls the last word out, and for the first time, I see *just* how intimidating she is. Don't get me wrong, Rosa always looks like she's one bad mood away from pulverising something. But this is the first time I've genuinely felt afraid of her.

Gulping, because I know I've fucked up, I timidly slip past a seething Rosa and head slowly downstairs. My feelings towards Allegra are not an excuse for going against her wishes. She asked me nicely to stay within the interior garden for my own safety and I ignored that.

I only know that's what I did because of the plant I plucked out of my hair. There are no vines in the interior garden. Granted, I was three sheets to the wind and have no recollection, but I shouldn't have put myself in a vulnerable position like that in the first place.

If I apologise quickly, maybe Allegra won't shoot me on sight. "I'm sorry," I bark as soon as I enter the room.

Allegra is sitting at her desk looking at something on her computer. She ignores me for a second and continues to click away. Finally, after I think I'm going to have a stroke, she looks up and pushes away from the desk slightly.

"Not looking too bright this morning, Bonnie."

At least we're not back to the Ms Moorside thing. Then I really would have panicked.

"I'm sure you'll be happy to know I feel like death warmed up."

"Believe it or not, that doesn't make me happy at all." Huh, okay.

"I'm genuinely sorry. I don't know why I went wherever I went."

"You took an evening stroll to the edge of our territory. I found you collapsed on the ground. You were metres away from the edge of a fucking cliff." Even though she swears, it's not rage I hear but...anxiety. She was worried about me.

"Bloody hell. I...don't remember any of it."

She goes silent for a second; her gaze drifting to the large window to her right. "Will you sit?"

I do as I'm told for two reasons. First, I think I might collapse if I don't park my bum. And second, because Allegra looks so tired. Again. It's the same look she had when I first arrived.

When she turns back to me, I'm a little stunned by her eyes. The two colours get me every time. I've read plenty of books where one character thinks another character's eyes are arresting and I never really got it. I mean, eyes are eyes, right? I get it now.

"We don't know each other, Bonnie. But I have a sense these past few days have been out of character for you."

Damn, she's noticed.

"At first, I was happy you were relaxing. Better than us constantly at each other's throats."

I nod, because yeah, holding all that rage is knackering, even though sometimes the conversational sparring kind of did it for me.

"I'm sure you want to tell me to fuck off, or some other basic insult. I get it."

"Actually, I agree with you," I reply.

Her brows hitch slightly. "Okay. Glad we're past the constant battles then. That being said, you might not feel that way after I've said my piece."

"Try me." I know what's coming, and I'm not mad. A little touched, actually.

"You're coping with being here by getting blackout drunk and it's not healthy. Your friend Pete is enabling you, and frankly, I'm ready to tear into him. What happened last night could have ended in disaster. Either you could have fallen, or someone could have attacked you. Neither are acceptable. I need you to stop. I understand being here is the last thing you want. But I need you to just help me to help you by staying safe and within the boundaries of the villa."

I swallow thickly because I still have no moisture in my body. "You know what my parents do?" This is the first time I feel comfortable having a conversation with her. She nods. "I grew up learning how to analyse my feelings and behaviour. When I woke up this morning, I scared myself. I've never been so drunk before I've blacked out. I didn't like it. There's a reason I'm a two-drink kinda girl. So I did a little self-reflection and came to the same conclusion as you."

She's doing that thing again, where she just looks at me.

"You were quite candid last night," she says.

Not the answer I was expecting. My stomach rolls, and it's not from the alcohol. What the hell did I say?

"Do I owe you another apology?"

She squints, and I see the beginning of a smirk. Shit.

"That depends. Were you lying when you called me Sexy Allegra?"

Oh, Jesus Christ on a paddleboard.

"Uh, I mean no... I'm not blind. You're attractive...in a felonious way." No point in trying to bullshit my way out of that one.

"Hmm. Felonious. Like a mafia queen, you might say?"

Dear God, no.

"What?" I squeak.

"A mafia queen you absolutely will not marry."

"I…"

"Although the sex slave idea was interesting. But I'm a baddie, so I doubt that will pan out."

I need her to stop talking. I can't remember anything, and I've decided I don't want to be reminded.

"I was very drunk!" It's my only argument. Clearly my booze-addled brain decided to word-vomit all my thoughts.

"Hmm. So, just to clarify, you won't marry me and become a queen consort?" Her eyes are sparkling with mirth, and I'm so embarrassed, the only thing I can do is burst out laughing. Which in turn sets Allegra off. I've heard her chuckle like a Disney villain, but this, her real laugh, is… Well, it's sweet.

"I'm so sorry," I cackle. "I can't stop imagining you, all gruff and tough, dealing with me being that drunk."

It's true. The thought of steel-faced Allegra Malgeri having to listen to my drunken twittering is hilarious. What did her face look like when I spouted all that crap?

"It was a first. But you were rather entertaining."

Wiping the tears from my eyes, I pull myself together a little. "I think I'm so dehydrated I've slipped into delirium." My shoulders are still shaking with laughter.

Allegra rolls her eyes before slipping from her chair and opening a door in the cupboard by the window. She pulls out a fresh bottle of water from what I presume is a small fridge. "Drink."

I drain the entire bottle in just a few gulps. "Thank you. And I promise, that will be the last time you have to deal with me in such a state."

She inclines her head. "Good."

She sits back down, and I can tell she has something else to say but is strangely shy about spilling the beans. I sit quietly and wait; a trick taught to me by my dads.

"I, uh, I wanted to say, I'm not a baddie, you know. Despite what you think."

I wasn't expecting that. She looks genuinely put out by my assessment of her. In all fairness, though, it was a drunken judgement. Sort of. I recall calling her the Devil in my head earlier. When she first took me from the bookstore, I *did* think she was a baddie, especially after the whole "Kelley getting shot" thing. But whether it's my raging hormones or something else, deep down, I know she's not the person she likes everyone to think. I could be blowing smoke up my own arse with those thoughts. Like she said, we don't know each other.

Mob's Seduction flitters to mind, and I internally cringe. I'm doing such a crappy job of resisting her villainous lure. No matter how many times I shout at myself, I feel pulled to Allegra. But is it due to her bad girl image, or could I have developed a real connection to the woman that stole me from my life?

16

Allegra

A CORNER HAS BEEN turned. Bonnie and I may never be best friends, but I think she'll stop fighting me every step of the way now. At least it puts my mind at ease knowing a repeat performance of her drunken wandering ways is unlikely.

She surprised me by opening up a little. It takes a strong person to look inwards. Bonnie has obviously learned from the best. I'm sure her fathers had her practising self-analysis by the time she could walk. It makes me envious. Self-reflection is hard, especially when you don't like what you see.

In this line of work and this type of family, it's not something easily practised. The times I try to navigate my behaviours and feelings usually leave me feeling torn, and I don't know what to do with that. I wish I were as confident as Bonnie. She came in here thinking I was going to tear into her. She held her head high, apologised, and showed a level of self-awareness I could only dream of.

Satisfied Bonnie is safe, and probably back in bed sleeping off her hideous hangover, I contemplate my next move. Rosa has been dealt with. Her lack of attention last night was inexcusable. She took my anger and apologised. Neglecting her post to screw one of the local girls almost came at a deadly cost. I doubt she'll make that mistake again.

My remaining issue lies with Pete and Kelley. Not so much Kelley, because I think she's a bit of a sheep—follows the crowd. In this case, Pete is the crowd. He's the one I take umbrage with. I don't have to know him well to get the measure of him. He uses avoidance tactics to deal with anything emotional: alcohol, men, parties; they are all used as an escape.

Now, I couldn't give a flying fuck if that's *his* go-to method; until it affects Bonnie, that is. She's under my protection, and Pete put her at serious risk last night. I know he was the one feeding her sugary cocktails. I've done my due diligence. That's how I found out Rosa was preoccupied with a good time rather than watching over our guests.

So, what to do? I'm sure Bonnie would prefer I do nothing, but that's impossible. Unless Pete is put in his place, he'll continue to encourage reckless behaviour. And that simply will not do.

Taking the gun from its holster, I place it in the safe below my desk. I want to have an honest talk with the man, and arriving with a pistol strapped to my waist will only put him on edge. Although, he's several cocktails in, so I'm sure he is already buzzed. Regardless, I don't need a gun to look formidable. Resting bitch face is its own weapon.

Making my way to the pool area, I mentally run through the meetings I have later. The most important by far, is with three other family heads: Francesco Luca, Nico Bosetti and Marco De Salvo. Together we make up the Sicilian Mafiosi. Giani Arello too, but he's the reason I want the meeting.

Between worrying about Bonnie, Lorenzo, the vineyard, and the import business, I've concluded I need to bring the other houses in on my predicament. Giani isn't someone I can deal with in secret.

His attempt to lure me into a ridiculous vengeance war is proof of that. His backhanded tactics have been low-grade, so far, but my gut tells me he's ready to escalate.

Simply threatening and seeking out Bonnie is proof of that. If I go toe-to-toe with him, without the other families being aware of the situation, I risk Giani spinning a story that puts the Ferrante family in the wrong. I've worked too hard to let that happen. Frankly, I don't have the time for it. Our businesses are flourishing and we are almost at the point where, if we wanted to, the family could extract itself from the Mafiosi entirely—a discussion Lorenzo and I need to have.

My unrest and ill at ease are becoming harder to ignore. Like I said, meeting Bonnie has somehow changed things for me. If I were able to analyse myself as well as she can, I'm sure I'd have an answer as to why. But I can't—not yet. Too many things feel like they're changing, and I need to deal with one crisis at a time.

I arrive at the pool with a million things whipping through my mind. That is, until I spot Pete basking in the sun, music blaring, drinking generously from a glass which contains a blue concoction that is likely ninety percent alcohol.

He's unaware of my presence. I stand and study him for a moment. Pete Bolton: thirty-six years old, lives in rented accommodation with his flatmate Lisa, and met Bonnie in school, where, to his credit, he befriended her and became her protector. When Bonnie left for university, Pete drifted from one bar job to the next, never really finding his place. He still spends his time living like he's a twenty-year-old student. He's had no serious relationships. One-night stands are his flavour. He's a ship without an anchor.

Adjusting my collar, I take the last two strides over to the portable speaker he loves so much. He spins and glares at me as soon as I stop the wretched noise. His glare turns into something else when he realises who it is he's trying to intimidate. My hair is in its severe bun, and my clothes are immaculate and imposing. How a blouse and slacks are able to intimidate someone I'm not sure, but I've been told enough times my attire adds to the overall "bad bitch" vibe.

"Mr Bolton, may I have a word?" It's not like me to ask, and in reality, I'm not seeking his permission, but I am cognisant of the fact he is one of Bonnie's best friends. If I put a foot wrong here, our newly developed ceasefire may fracture, and we'll be back to trading vicious barbs before we reach dinner.

He sits up and has the decency to cover his barely there swim trunks with a towel. How anyone finds the male species attractive is beyond me.

"Of course," he stumbles.

"We've not been formally introduced. I'm Allegra Malgeri."

"P-Pete Bolton."

I take the time to perch regally on the adjacent sunbed. Chiara, the house chef, cocks her brow at me through the kitchen window. She makes the universal sign for drink. As much as I'd love a glass of wine, it's far too early and I don't want Pete to think we will ever be that friendly. I give her a subtle head shake.

"I'd like to discuss yesterday's events."

"With me?" he asks, confused.

"Yes, with you. I've been led to believe your idea of helping Bonnie through what is a traumatic and life-altering time, is to ply her with enough alcohol to fell a horse."

"I... But..."

"You must know I see everything, Mr Bolton. This is my house, and you are my guests. Now, I won't excuse Bonnie. She's an adult, after all, and makes her own decisions, however, I've been watching you, Mr Bolton. I've watched you encourage her relentlessly."

"Hey, hang on. You don't know me or Bonnie."

"Oh, but I do. I know Bonnie would rather sit with a good book and maybe a small glass of wine. I know she's a two-drink kind of woman, and I know this past week has thrown her entire life into the air. I know she looks to you for protection. I know you haven't lived up to that job for a while now. And I know that instead of helping her work through this, you've decided to take the easy way out and get her drunk every hour of the day."

"I'm not her keeper," he protests.

"No, you are supposed to be her best friend. She begged to have you here because the thought of anything happening to you was unfathomable. I agreed. I'm seriously regretting that decision. Last night wasn't just some silly drunken escapade. Bonnie could have got seriously hurt—killed even—and yet here you are, back by the pool, drinking, instead of checking on your friend. Even Kelley crawled out of bed to make sure she was fine. And thanks to me finding her, she is."

"I tried to see her last night, but you—"

"I would have shot you if I'd stopped. You are skating through life telling Bonnie how boring she is. You have the audacity to pick apart her choices when you're here, being a man-child, with no direction or prospects. Bonnie might enjoy books over beer. Microwave meals over clubbing. But at least she's content. Can you say the same, Mr Bolton?" His mouth bobs open and shut. "No, I didn't think so. With that said, I suggest you refrain from 'helping' Bonnie until you can offer her more than this—until you can be the person she needs. Oh, and one last thing: If I hear you have been encouraging her to drink her worries away again, I'll have you thrown to the wolves, regardless of Bonnie's wishes. *Capiche?*"

There, I feel much better now. I don't wait to hear an answer. I've made myself clear. Now I need to shift focus onto the rest of my day. The meeting with the family heads is in a few hours, so I have two options: sit at my desk and pore through finances or take a stroll over to the farmhouse I am having renovated. My plan is to open a restaurant that serves our wine and local food. It's been in the pipeline for several years and it's finally almost a reality.

Stepping out of the villa, I take in the view and a large breath of sea air. The restaurant is a five-minute walk. We have quad bikes and golf carts, but I never use them. Why would anyone want to rush here? Time in the vineyard is precious.

Laughter greets me as I step through the restaurant door. The interior is almost finished and it looks divine. The aesthetic is in line with the villa's authentic look and feel, but it also boasts top-of-the-line equipment. The kitchen is a chef's wet dream.

In the corner of the main restaurant area sits Lorenzo, sipping a glass of red with Mark and Phillip. They seem to be getting on well, and Lorenzo certainly looks happier. I'm a little irritated at them too, to be honest. While they've been getting to know each other, Bonnie has been struggling. I can't imagine it has escaped her fathers' attentions. So why haven't they intervened? Maybe I should find out. I've already set one arrogant shit straight today. Might as well make it three more.

"Gentlemen," I say in greeting. "Enjoying yourselves?"

"Ah, Allegra. How are you, *tesoro*?"

"Busy."

Lorenzo laughs. "Always on the go, my Allegra," he says to Mark and Phillip. "We decided to give the kids some space. Let them enjoy the villa."

I nod and eye them carefully. "So much space you missed Bonnie's drunk excursion to the edge of our property last night."

"Our Bonnie?" Mark replies.

"Or the days before, where she hasn't been sober for a second."

"She's letting off some steam," Phillip quips.

I have reached my limit for dealing with bullshit today. Standing with hands on hips, I level a stare at them that could melt glass. "What the fuck is wrong with you all?" I hiss.

Bonnie's dads look taken aback. Lorenzo carefully puts his glass on the table.

"Your daughter," I say, pointing at each of them, Lorenzo included. "Is lost. She was kidnapped—by me, witnessed a shooting, met her biological father, discovered there is a mob family after her, and was taken out of the country. You think she's just letting off steam? Do you know her at all? Why am I the only one giving a shit? While you three have been playing Dad of the Year Club, Bonnie has been drowning herself in booze, no thanks to her ass of a friend, Pete. She got so drunk last night she blacked out. Is that just her letting off steam, too?"

As with Pete, the three dipshits look at me agog. "How about you stop whatever the hell this is, and go make sure your child is okay? How about someone here, apart from me, give a damn that we have effectively trashed this poor woman's life!"

I can't look at their faces anymore. I storm out and march back to my office. Guilt rolls around my gut. As much as I rant and rave at everyone, at the end of the day,

Bonnie's mental distress lands at *my* feet. It's my fault. And I don't know how to undo it.

Maybe I *am* the baddie she believes me to be. I scoff. *Of course I am.*

17

Bonnie

THERE HAVE BEEN SEVERAL things that have left me speechless over the past week, and none of them compared to hearing Allegra rip into Pete and then my parents; Lorenzo too. It still doesn't feel right giving him a parental title.

After our talk in her office, I had every intention of going to bed and sleeping until the next day. Pete put pay to that by listening to music far too loud. I was already leaning out my window to give him an earful when I watched Allegra walk over and switch off the music player. I probably should have closed the window and minded my own business, but I was curious. I couldn't think of a reason for Allegra to speak with Pete.

I listened as Allegra calmly berated Pete. My first instinct was to rush to his defence, but I was frozen, unable to utter a sound. As soon as she finished, the world began to spin again, and I found myself rushing to the stairs with every intention of having some stern words of my own. After all, I didn't need her fighting my battles—battles I wasn't convinced were necessary. I mean, sure, Pete encouraged me to stop being dull and live a little, but it was my choice. Granted, any time I tried to talk about how I was feeling, Pete shut the conversation down and shoved another drink in my hand, but it was me who chose to take it.

With Allegra's added height, her pace was far beyond mine. I had to jog to catch up when I finally saw the direction she'd taken. I was wrong to guess she'd head back to her office. When I found her, she'd stepped into a beautiful building, fresh from renovation.

Once again, I stepped in, ready to have a row with her, but was pinned to the spot. Allegra was standing by a table with my dads and Lorenzo. Her voice was more dangerous than it had been with Pete. I listened to her again and was floored. The woman I'd called the Devil was fighting everyone...for me and my well-being.

The second she huffed out a frustrated breath, I knew she was about to turn and walk in my direction. The adult in me said I should have stayed put and faced it head-on, but as evidenced by my recent behaviour, I was struggling with the concept of adulting as a whole. So I tucked tail and rounded the corner of the building until I was sure she was gone and I could emerge unseen.

I ran straight into my dads, who still looked a little shell-shocked. And this is where I am now; standing in front of my dads without a clue how to approach what I just heard.

"Bonnie," Pop squeaks. His voice always gets high when he's stressed.

"I heard her," I reply, because I can't lie to them.

Dad looks to the ground and nods to himself. It's funny how people do that: nod to themselves or shake their heads. Why I'm contemplating that now, I don't know, but it's an interesting facet of human behaviour.

"Did you hear me, sweetheart?" Dad says.

I didn't hear him because my brain hasn't been able to linger on a single thought all day. It's like a racecourse up there. Whichever thought pulls ahead is what I latch on to, whether it's appropriate for the moment or not...just like now. I still haven't answered him.

"Sorry, Dad, I was miles away. What did you say?"

He takes me by the shoulders. "I asked if you'd come and sit with us for a second."

"Oh, sure, in there?" I ask, pointing to the restaurant.

"How about the bench under the olive tree?" Pop says. It doesn't take a rocket scientist to know he doesn't want me within a mile of alcohol.

Following close behind, I can't help but cast a glance over at the villa. What is she doing now?

Sitting between my dads, I hold up my hand. "Before we start, please know I have recognised my pattern of behaviour and understand how destructive it is. I will have a drink, but only when I feel like it, and with food. I learned my lesson after last night."

They take my hands and squeeze. "We know, honey. We trust your judgement. But we should have been more present. Allegra was right. We should have known better and stepped in earlier. We're sorry, my love." Dad is so sincere it almost breaks my heart.

"Your dad's right, pumpkin. It's been a whirlwind of change and surprises. We shouldn't have presumed you could cope with it all alone."

"Thank you. I...I'm struggling. You know me. I like routine. My life is exactly as I want it, and this has effectively thrown a grenade in the centre of my world."

Dad smooths my hair behind my ear. "Tell us what you need, honey, and we'll do everything in our power to help."

What do I need? Time, I guess. Nothing I say or do changes the fact Lorenzo is my father or that I'm here.

"I need to process it. You've been spending a lot of time with Lorenzo. Is...is he nice?"

They exchange a look. "We wanted to know the man that made you, pumpkin. And we wanted to hear about your mother. Maybe that was wrong of us. After all, you should be the one finding these things out before us. I'm sorry, love."

"We're messing this up, huh, kid?"

I shake my head. "I don't think there's a right or wrong way. You guys are going through your own stuff. I get it."

"But you come first, Bonnie. Always. If it's making you uncomfortable, say the word and we'll stick to the villa like hermits."

I chuckle, "No, it's fine. I...I think I should talk to Lorenzo. Maybe then I won't feel so trapped in my head about it all, you know?"

"I think that's a wise decision," Dad says. "I know Lorenzo would like the opportunity. But you don't owe it to him, so only do it if it's what you really want."

I nod. My mind goes to Allegra again and a small smile creeps its way to my face. "She shouted at Pete, too." I giggle. "Allegra, that is."

Pop sits back and laughs. "I think we all deserved it."

"She's not what I thought." I didn't mean to say that out loud.

"Hmm, in what way?" Dad is in therapist mode.

I shrug. "I thought she was horrible to begin with. Nothing but a criminal. A baddie."

"And now?" Pop joins in with his soothing, lay-on-the-couch-and-tell-me-all-your-woes voice.

Another shrug. "She was mean in the beginning. I stand by that. But I think there's more to her—to this place—than I realise. It's not like it is in my books."

"It never is, sweetie. But," Dad sighs, "be mindful she is still a criminal, even if her attitude has changed. That goes for Lorenzo, too."

"Dad's right. We're stuck here for the time being, and I think it *is* healthy for you to explore your past. But one day, hopefully not too long from now, all this will be over and we will go home. Lorenzo and Allegra will resume whatever it is they do. Maybe leaving a little space is wise."

"We don't want you to get hurt or put in danger, ever again, love," Dad adds.

I know they're right. My opinion on Allegra might have changed from when we met, but at the end of it all, she's still a mob queen, and Lorenzo is still the Don of a mob family.

We hug it out and I assure my dads they can leave me alone with my thoughts. My solitary pondering is soon interrupted by a fully clothed Pete. It's going to be one of those days that will leave me emotionally drained. I can feel it.

"Hey, Bon," he says quietly.

"Hey, Pete. You okay?"

He gives me a boop on the nose. "I just had my ass whooped by Allegra."

I like that he never beats around the bush.

"Hmm, I heard."

He plonks himself down next to me and wraps one of his giant arms around my shoulders. "Sorry, Bonnie. I've been a totally shit friend, haven't I?"

"No, you haven't."

"Yeah, I have." He pulls me closer. "Can I tell you something?"

I lay my head on his shoulder. "Always."

"She's right. About it all. I'm skating through life without a fucking clue. I'm really lost, Bonnie, and I don't know how to deal with it or change anything, so I've just been repeating the same thing over and over."

"Why didn't you say anything?" I ask. I don't turn to look at him because he wouldn't cope with that kind of attention. The fact he's finally opening up is enough.

"You've always had your shit together, Bon, even when we were kids. You knew what you wanted and went for it. I never had that clarity. I thought as I got older it would magically hit me—what I wanted out of life—but it never happened. I'm jealous of you, actually."

Now I *do* turn and look at him. "What on earth are you talking about?"

He laughs and pulls me back until my head is back on his shoulder. "You're content, Bonnie. You've made a life you're happy with."

"A boring life," I mutter.

"No," he begins, and I can feel him shaking his head, "I mean, yeah, you could do with getting out a little more, but nothing like I've been prattling on about. You are a home bird. You love reading, and you've got great friends and a job that allows you to fulfil your passion. You've never liked drinking and clubbing, and frankly, it's shit. It's the same people—the same drama."

"So why do it?"

He flaps his lips as he lets out a big breath. "Because it's what I know. Change is really fucking hard, and I wouldn't know what to do, anyway."

"We can figure it out, Pete. I'm here for you, just as much as you've always been for me. You don't always have to be the protector."

"I know. And after this shitshow is over, I promise I'll ask for help. In the meantime, I need to know how you're doing. Seriously."

"I'm getting there. I've got stuff to work through, and I know I will."

"Of course you will. Is Kelley okay?"

"I think so. Ugh, maybe *I* need to start being a better friend, too. If anyone should be traumatised, it's her, but she's spent her time making sure I'm okay."

"I think we all need to do better. How about we go find her and spend some time talking. No alcohol."

We stand up and hug each other. I needed this; the talk with my dads and Pete. I might be tired with all the analysing and deep, thought-provoking conversation, but ignoring the issue isn't for me. I just needed Allegra to give me a kick up the bum, apparently, because as much as it was about her calling out the men in my life, she's made me see I need to open up and let them in; ask for their help instead of waiting for it to be offered. She also helped me see I need to step up my friendship game, too.

We drag Kelley out of bed and spend the rest of the day talking. It's not all heavy, but we end the day with a group hug and a promise to do better. Pete and Kelley head to their rooms first. My mind is still on a fast track, so I tell them I'm going for a walk. I have to promise them I'm not going to wander off again before they leave me alone.

The sky shines with thousands of stars as I slowly meander around the interior garden. I don't know a rose from a teapot, so I can't admire the garden with the attention it deserves. I just know the flowers look pretty. The crickets are chirping loudly and there is a light breeze. It really is a perfect night.

A thought enters my mind, and I don't know what to make of it. As I'm standing here, enjoying the sights and sounds of Sicily, I think there is only one thing that could make it even better.

Allegra.

Yeah, I'm in trouble.

18

Allegra

MIA DRIVES STEADILY DOWN the dirt road. For once, I'd like to meet in a bar or restaurant, but as you can imagine, the heads of four crime families gathering together draws attention.

I have to be content meeting Francesco, Nico, and Marco in an abandoned building several kilometres from the villa. It could be worse. They also could have refused the meeting, so I'll take what I can get.

Three SUVs are lined up when we arrive. No doubt the three Dons are exchanging stories, each vying to make their dick feel bigger than the others. It's always a pissing contest with these people. Mia scans the area as usual. I'm not worried about my safety. I'm packing and I have no bad blood with anyone here, but I appreciate her vigilance.

The air is thick with cigar smoke when I walk in, and sure enough, Marco, Nico, and Francesco are talking over each other, trying to make themselves seem important. It's so tiring.

"Gentlemen, sorry I'm late." I'm not late, and even if I were, I wouldn't be sorry, but it's how the game goes. I've had to work twice as hard to earn their respect because I have a vagina. I've done the dance long enough to know which hill I'm willing to die on, and this ain't it. Let them think I give a shit about their judgement of me. It's no skin off my nose.

"Allegra, good to see you," Francesco bellows. He has no volume control.

"Good to see you, too. All of you. Shall we get down to it?"

I have no intention of staying here a second longer than necessary. The building is dilapidated to the point I'm sure it's unsafe.

"Indeed. We're all wondering why you've called the meeting," Nico says. "And not invited Giani," he adds.

"Then I'll speak plainly. Giani is attempting to draw the Ferrante family into a war."

"And why would he do that?" Marco asks. His hair is slicked back and he always wears way too much cologne.

It's like he watched *The Godfather* one too many times and decided he had to emulate everything about it.

"Thirty-odd years ago, Lorenzo had an affair with a woman called Maria. She was intended to marry Giani. Maria became pregnant, and for her safety and that of the baby's, Lorenzo had them hidden. In short, Giani has never gotten over it."

"I'm surprised Fenza allowed Lorenzo to keep his balls," Nico laughs.

"She didn't know. No one knew. Well, that is until Giani threatened Lorenzo's long-lost daughter's life. Somehow, he found out. We've dealt with his attempts on our shipments. But coming after a family member is crossing the line. She's an innocent bystander. Because of Giani, she's had her life ripped away and is in hiding."

Marco shakes his head. "We can't get involved, Allegra, you know that."

"I'm not asking you to. I just wanted to fill you in, so if something were to happen, Giani can't paint a picture that favours him. I have no intention of fighting him."

"And what does Lorenzo want? He's still the Don, isn't he?" Nico asks. It's a barb that's meant to prick me, but it doesn't. Nothing these men say has that kind of power.

"Lorenzo is Don in name only. You know that, so cut the shit. I make the decisions." As much as I've run the family from the shadows, the three other Dons have known for some time.

"She is fiery, isn't she?" Francesco grins. "You make a fine Donna, Allegra."

I bow my head in recognition of his compliment. He doesn't give them out often.

"If what you say is true, and Giani is messing with your shipments, you already have cause to—"

"It's what he wants," I say impatiently. Why am I having to explain this? "Giani thinks I'm stupid enough to let his silly little attempts on our cargo sway my decision. He wants a war, and it's even better if I look to be the one starting it. I couldn't give a fuck about his three-decade-old grudge. We're better than that. However, if he makes an attempt on Bonnie, that's a different matter. You would all be obliged to step in."

Nico taps the table with his lighter. "If the Arellos cross that line, we will assist you. Our pact remains strong. Our businesses are thriving because we've looked out for each other. None of us can afford petty jealousy to unravel our hard work."

I refrain from telling them that our pact means little to me, not in the way they think. Yes, it served as a security blanket when Lorenzo took over from his father. It allowed him to train me and start changing the way our family operated, but since I've taken the helm, we don't need the pact as much as the others. They still run most of their businesses from underground. Nico is the drug kingpin of Italy. Francesco traffics weapons, and Marco dabbles in everything.

The pact states that no family in the Mafiosi can willingly harm another member's family or business. The pact forbids wars over land and business territories. We keep each other's secrets, therefore ensuring our survival. And it's worked.

"Nico is right. If Giani takes this further, we'll have no choice but to get involved. Keep us updated, Allegra," Francesco replies, "and tell Lorenzo to call. It's been too long."

"Of course, and thank you. Until the next time." We shake hands and part ways. As far as meetings go, it was short but effective. I've cut Giani off at the knees and he doesn't even know it yet. One wrong move from him and he'll effectively wipe his own family name off the map.

Once the Mafiosi are involved, it's as good as a signed death warrant.

That's not what I want. I've seen far too much death to last a lifetime. I would never wish that on anyone. Giani is a bastard, but he has children and grandchildren. The only thing that would come of his death, is more violence. We left that behind a long time ago, so I need this to end peacefully.

The sun is setting as Mia drives us back to the villa. "Mia, can we make a pit stop, please?" I'm suddenly craving Mamma Picollo's famous pasta. She's a legend in these parts and I'm ashamed to say it's been far too long since I've seen her.

Mia doesn't need me to give her instructions. She knows what I mean when I say "pit stop". My stomach rumbles as we approach the small restaurant nestled in between houses. If you didn't know it was there, you'd miss it entirely. Mamma Picollo has been running the restaurant for nearly sixty years. Her family has always been in the food industry, one way or another.

Thanking Mia, I hop out of the car and push through the door. The comforting embrace of heavenly smelling food calms me instantly. I chuckle when I hear Mamma Picollo shouting at someone in the back. She might be in her eighties, but she's as prickly as a cactus and takes shit from no one.

A few bangs and clangs of pots filter through the dining area. No one bats an eyelash. Everyone here is a local and knows Mamma Picollo. She's like everyone's grandmother. I sit at my favourite table at the back. It has a permanent *reserved* sign just for me.

"Well, look who decided to pop up her head and say hello!" Mamma Picollo barks. My smile is a mile long as I stand and take the tiny woman in my arms. She smells like Parmesan and love.

"*Ciao, Mamma*," I whisper into her hair.

She pushes me away and assesses me like usual. "You need to eat more, *Bella*. You're skin and bones."

She's said the same thing to me every time I've seen her for the past twenty-five years.

"I eat plenty," I say. Although recently, my stomach has revolted at the thought of food. There's just too much stress.

"Sit, sit. I'll bring you food," she babbles, pushing me down to the chair. I gave up trying to order a dish many years ago. Mamma Picollo knows best, according to her, so she chooses what I'll eat. No doubt it will be enough to feed the entire family, so I'll have most of it put in doggy bags to take home.

Sitting here in low candlelight, as I listen to the chaos of the kitchen reminds me of simpler times. Mamma Picollo's was the place to find me when I was a kid and needed space. She doted on me like I was her own grandchild, and I needed that at times, especially if Lorenzo pissed me off. I'd go running to Mamma Picollo and she'd make everything better with pasta and a hug.

As predicted, I'm served several dishes. I get a scornful look when I barely finish one, even though it was huge. I ask to have the rest bagged up and I promise to visit again soon.

Maybe I could bring Bonnie?

Only because she might need a bit of space, of course.

I hand Mia one of Mamma Picollo's cannoli and she dramatically clutches her chest telling me how much she loves me, which makes me laugh. For the first time in a long time, I feel lighter. That's the wonder of Mamma Picollo.

As we pull up to the villa, I spot Bonnie meandering through the flowers. I know I should leave her alone and go about my business, but my legs have other ideas. Before I know it, I'm only a few feet away, holding up the food bag.

"Hi. Do you want food?"

She looks at me, startled. Her eyes bounce from the bag to my face. "Um...hi. And wow, what is that smell?"

I grin. "That is the smell of the best food in Italy." I don't even mind saying it with Chiara close by because she would agree. "I've got far too much, and you should experience Mamma Picollo's before you leave."

Nope, my body doesn't like that thought at all!

I turn and start walking back to the villa. Bonnie hesitates for a second but then follows. Placing the bag on the counter, I set about collecting plates and bowls. Bonnie will have a veritable feast.

"This looks...incredible," she says, leaning over and inhaling deeply.

"Taste it. Then your mind will *really* be blown," I chuckle. Even though I'm stuffed to the brim, I could eat a little more. We fall silent as we eat. No, not silent, because Bonnie is making appreciative noises that should be made illegal. Does she know she's doing it?

She's so captivating I've stopped eating, my fork halfway to my mouth. Only when her eyes flash open and she catches me staring, do I finally look away, trying not to choke on my food.

We go a few more minutes without speaking and they're the loudest minutes of my life. My skin feels itchy and my hair is too tight. Reaching up, I yank it out of the bun. No one should endure that torture every day. I don't have to, but I learned early how the more severe look earned me more respect. Ridiculous, I know, but that's the patriarchy for you.

When I look up, Bonnie is staring at me still. The air feels charged and I can't tell if it's a good thing or not. Is she planning to lay into me about something?

"I don't get you," she finally says. "Who are you?"

I feel my eyebrows draw together because I'm not sure what she means, but I don't have time to formulate a question.

"One minute you're this terrifying ice queen—the mobster—but on the flip side, you're this," she says, waving her hand at me. "Laughing. Laid back. Caring. You're like night and day and I don't understand."

Laying my fork down, I dab my mouth with a napkin. There is no easy way to answer her. It's far too long and complicated, but something inside urges me to tell her everything about who I am. If it means she'll stop seeing me as the Devil incarnate, it's worth it, right?

19

Bonnie

I WAS RIGHT. ALLEGRA turning up out of the blue with a bag full of scrumptious food has made the night perfect—also, confounding. I just can't get a handle on her and it's messing with my head.

My dad's warning is rattling around my noggin, telling me to eat my food and go to bed. She's a criminal no matter how I cut it. Nothing she does or says changes that, and yet, I've not followed anyone's advice and eaten and gone to bed. Instead, I've opened my trap and blurted out my innermost thoughts.

"What do you want to know?" she says.

Um, everything? But I don't want to come across as too eager.

I set my own cutlery down. "Lorenzo raised you, I guess?"

"He did. My parents were killed by a rival family and he took me in."

I knew it was something along those lines.

"And so, what? He trained you to be...this?" I don't know how to describe her. "Evil mobster" doesn't sound right, but I know she's far from innocent.

She taps the end of a finger to her chin. "Okay, Bonnie, I'll tell you my sad little story and you can decide if I'm worth your time."

Oh, that was ice cold.

Shaking my head, I reach over and lay my hand over hers. "I'm sorry. I didn't mean... You *are* worth my time, Allegra." And she is. I know it.

"This is the only world I've ever known, Bonnie. Believe it or not, Lorenzo did everything in his power to change how the family did business, but we are rooted in decades worth of tradition and it takes time. You may not agree with this," she says, brandishing her arms wide, "but do not be foolish enough to think we are the only bad guys. It's not so black and white. Do you know how many law enforcement officials, politicians, and heads of state are involved in our line of work? They just don't openly call themselves mobsters. We live in a world of dog-eat-dog. Maybe you should open your eyes and see the grey areas before you so easily judge me or Lorenzo—but I digress, Lorenzo loved me and cared for me, not with the sole purpose of raising me to be a criminal, as you so love to phrase it. He was the parent I needed; in the only way he knew how. I'm naturally gifted with numbers, so it was natural for me to fall into the business side of things as I got older. I wanted, and want, to make sure the family is secure. I owe the Ferrante name everything."

Fiddling with my knife, I look at her with a new purpose. She's right. I've judged her harshly. And rightly so in the beginning, but now, I'm seeing a different side of her life. Since being here, I haven't once seen or heard anything that is tantamount to brutal behaviour, which I absolutely thought would be the case.

In *Mob's Seduction* the family are out busting knees and cracking heads every night. The only thing happening here is a lot of hard work, mainly from the field pickers, and Allegra in her office.

"I know it... I don't... Okay, yes, I've judged you, but when we first met, I think you'll agree it wasn't the best first impression."

She grins. "I'll give you that. I came in far too strong. And I won't lie. There have been times I've had to be the woman you met that day. But not everyone is as innocent as you, Bonnie. The world is cruel. I've had to play the bitch to keep myself safe. Also," she shrugs, "I do like the rush. Being that powerful is an addiction. No point denying it."

I need to choose my words carefully because I don't want her to clam up. "But you've...you've hurt people before?"

She nods. "Yes. But I can promise you this: None of them were innocent. Some were cruel and I'll admit I enjoyed it at times. Those reasons may not excuse it in your eyes, but as I said, things are never black and white. Spilling blood meant I'd earned my way to where I am now. Growing up, reaching the head of the family was my only goal. I didn't have anything else."

"Okay. Do you...do you sell drugs?"

"No, never," she sighed. "Okay, I'm going to tell you something that could potentially get me killed."

"No!"

She holds up her hands. "You need to understand how this works, Bonnie, if you want your questions answered." She waits until I gesture for her to continue. "There are several families that make up the Mafiosi. Each family has a different stream of income. Drugs, guns, protection, and theft. The Ferrante family had their finger in the drug business at one point, but Lorenzo's father stopped it after a while. It's too volatile and messy. A pact was made between the families. It ensured there would be no turf wars or encroachment on each other's businesses. A refined way to live The Life; one far different from the Mafiosi of old."

Blimey, I feel like I should be taking notes.

"When I began to run the businesses here, I chose to focus on our legitimate sources of income. Times are changing and it won't be long before the law catches up to families like ours, no matter how many people we pay off. Because, Bonnie, there will always be a bigger fish out there, and they will come for us when it's advantageous for them. So I've built up a Ferrante empire that is beyond reproach. That being said, we still have one line of income that is less than legal."

"What is it?" Do I want to know? Does it make me an accessory?

"Art theft and forgery. We steal from the wealthy, only to sell it back to them."

Huh, okay, as far as crimes go, it's not so bad.

You're making excuses because you like Allegra!

Looking into her eyes, I can't lie to myself; I do like her. She's gorgeous and mysterious. Not so much now, but she'll always hold that air of forbidden fruit that tempts me so.

"That was a lot. Sorry, I don't know what to say now."

She starts eating and I see her walls rise again. "Nothing for you to say. I just hope I've shone a light on things you were finding difficult to understand."

"Thanks. You didn't owe me that. But I appreciate it, and it helps me see these different sides to you more clearly."

We fall silent and finish our meal. I'm not sure what I want to happen next. I don't want the evening to end, but what am I hoping to get out of it if it continues?

Allegra clears the dishes and wipes the counter. She's totally at home and happy here. It was the reason I asked her who she is. The second she took her hair down, it was like this other persona slotted into place and she became a woman at home, enjoying a meal. It was all so *normal*.

It's this side of her that has my heart racing as she moves around the kitchen. Sure, the bad girl vibe is hot, but that kind of thrill only leads to getting burned. This Allegra is so much more appealing. She's softer, and she's beautiful. Her eyes take on a glow that is so often missing when she's in boss mode.

Maybe that's what leads me to reach out and take her by the wrist as she goes to walk past me. Her skin is soft against my fingertips. I watch in trepidation as she stops and turns her head to me. I haven't got the answer to her earlier question. I don't know what I want, but my mouth opens before my brain engages.

"I don't think you're a baddie, Allegra."

"No? So who do you think I am?" Her voice wavers and I see how vulnerable I'm making her feel.

"I think you're beautiful." I could have said a thousand different things, but those words are what came out. And I don't want to take them back.

She turns her body to me. Now *I* feel vulnerable. For all I know, she's about to laugh in my face. I've seen a softer side, but I know the ice is never far away. She probably thinks I'm pathetic, getting mushy over the woman that took her, and she's probably right, but try telling that to the chemical reaction happening inside my body right now.

Allegra doesn't laugh. She takes a step towards me until her body is crammed between my legs. Her palms reach my face and I'm speechless. Any bravery I had has melted quicker than the cream in Mamma Picollo's cannoli.

Our eyes lock, and I couldn't look away now, even if I wanted to. I don't. Is she asking for permission? Without thinking, I nod, and her lips descend. But before I feel her mouth on mine, she whispers, "You're beautiful too...*out of wool.*"

And then Allegra Malgeri, crime boss extraordinaire, is kissing me like the world is about to end.

I'll admit my kissing experience isn't profound. Don't get me wrong; I've had some nice make-out sessions before. Not many, though, and nowhere near as explosive, fulfilling, and lust-inducing as this one. I'm shrouded in her scent and warmth. My hands travel to her hair because, apparently, I am all in. And her platinum locks have called to me from the very first time I saw her.

Scraping my fingers across her scalp, something primal takes over. I gather her tresses and pull, making her moan. This isn't me. I'm fiery in temper but never with a woman. I'm the "soft touches" kind of girl; the one who likes sweet and slow. Whoever the hell I am at this moment doesn't want any of that. No. I want her passion, and I want to show her mine.

A flick of her tongue across my lower lip has me opening my mouth to let her in. She delves in and immediately owns me. Her hands snake around me and grab my hips, pulling me closer until my crotch is firmly against her. I naturally start rocking because I just can't help myself. That is, until the bubble is shattered. We both hear Lorenzo's voice filter down the hallway, heading in our direction.

Allegra wrenches herself from me, looking half-crazed. I try to say something, but my throat closes up and she shakes her head. We set about straightening our clothes just in time. Lorenzo rounds the kitchen doorway with my dads in tow.

I see the flicker of recognition on my dads' faces. They know exactly what was happening seconds before they entered, and I can't stop my face from flaming. Lorenzo seems utterly oblivious, which I'm grateful for.

"Bonnie, Allegra, it's good to see you both," he says affably.

"Lorenzo, Mark, Phillip. I hope you've had a good day," Allegra replies, calm as a sodding cucumber. My heart is doing the Cha-Cha Slide, and I can hear blood pulsing through my ears.

"Very nice, thank you," Pops says. Dad is staying silent. Shit.

"We were just coming to grab a snack," Lorenzo prattles on. "Is that Mamma Picollo's?" he asks. Allegra nods. "Oh, it's been far too long."

"Feel free," she replies. Lorenzo doesn't wait to dig in. "If you'll excuse me." She gives me a quick, side-eyed glance and then leaves.

"Mark, Phillip, you absolutely need to taste this. Mamma Picollo is an institution around here."

I need the awkward stand-off to end right now. "You should, it's fantastic. Anyway, I'm off to bed."

"Bonnie," Dad begins, but I'm not doing this now. I've got to process that life-shattering kiss Allegra just planted on me. My dad's shock will have to wait.

"Tomorrow," I say with conviction. "Good night, Lorenzo. Maybe...um, maybe we could talk in the afternoon?"

Lorenzo stops chewing, and his eyes bulge. It's kind of funny. He rushes to chew and swallow, but he's already nodding his head.

"I'd love to. I'll be in the restaurant all afternoon."

I give him a smile and half a wave. "Okay, then. Night."

Glad to be out of there, I take the stairs two at a time and then freeze. Allegra is just down the hall from me. Is she thinking about that kiss? Did it affect her as much as it did me? Am I brave enough, or stupid enough, to go and find out?

20

Allegra

I ONCE TRAVELLED TO the States to meet a drug lord who was far too persistent in trying to get the Ferrante family back into the drug business. I turned up to that meeting with just my gun and Toni as back-up. I faced down that little arsehole and his crew of overgrown toddlers, without a flicker of apprehension.

That is the level of calm and control I have over myself—*had* over myself—until I kissed Bonnie. I'd rather take on a thousand drug cartels than feel this unnerved by that woman. No one has ever gotten to me like that; not even Petra.

But when Bonnie grabbed my wrist and looked at me the way she did, I was powerless to keep calm. My nerves became electricity pylons, and her attention sent them into overdrive until I short-circuited.

I've been called beautiful before, but the way Bonnie said it, after everything we've been through together, broke something in me. She wasn't telling me my body was beautiful; she was referring to something she sees in me—something I've never let anyone else see.

Even with Petra, I had to keep up a façade. She was a part of my world and knew what it took to be in a position of power. Maybe, deep down, I knew Petra wasn't a safe option to open myself up to.

It doesn't matter now. What's important is that I had my tongue in Bonnie's mouth and my hands on her hips. I expected her to push me back, maybe even strike me for being so presumptuous, but she didn't do those things. In fact, she grabbed my hair in a way that told me she was more than enjoying our shared experience. And then it was shattered by none other than her parents and Lorenzo.

She must be freaking out now. No doubt she'll ignore me in the morning or even hide from me. Of course, she'll realise what a monumental mistake it was to kiss the woman who shot her best friend.

My head shoots to the door when I hear a soft knock. It can't be. With hesitation, I reach for the handle. Maybe it's Mark or Phillip here to warn me off. They had clearly figured out what we were doing the second they laid eyes on us.

It's neither of Bonnie's dads.

"Bonnie," I say stupidly.

"Can I come in?" She's wringing her hands, clearly nervous. I step to the side and allow her to pass. I've only just shut the door when she's all up in my space. "You kissed me!"

"I did."

"Why?"

"I wanted to." It's like I'm on a game show and this is the quickfire round.

"You think I'm beautiful?"

"Yes."

"But not in wool?" Why on earth is that something to focus on? I'd said it as a joke...kind of.

"You are beautiful no matter what. I just don't care for the material."

This is bizarre, but I'll play along if that's what Bonnie needs.

"You took my clothes."

"I did."

"I like the ones you gave me, and that makes me mad."

"Okay. Sorry."

"No, you're not."

"Okay, I'm not."

She's so close I could pull her into me in a second and claim those delicious lips again, but I restrain my urge. Bonnie is working through something, and I don't want to ruin my chances by doing something stupid.

"I wanted to kiss you, too."

"You should hate me," I say. It's true. She *should* hate me—everything about me—and I don't understand why she doesn't. I know I explained how things work around here, but I didn't think for a second, she would suddenly go from her original judgements to...this. "Unless..."

"Unless?"

It suddenly occurs to me that Bonnie's recent behaviour may indicate this is a revenge thing. I know the kiss in the kitchen would have led to sex if we'd not been interrupted. It's more than likely Bonnie was subconsciously trying to hate-fuck me. Just like her drinking, it's a way for her to cope. And the thought sends acid shooting to my throat. How could I have been so stupid?

"Allegra," she says, her eyes boring into me.

"It's okay," I say, "I understand."

"Well, that's fantastic. Care to fill me in because I haven't got a bloody clue what you're talking about."

"Bonnie, there is no chance on this earth you like me that way. Look how we started."

"So, for what reason do you think I was kissing you?"

I shrug. "A hate-fuck is a great way to take back power."

I regret it the second I say it because the look on her face is one I never want to see again. She takes a step back but doesn't say a word. It's my turn to wring my hands.

"Sit on the bed," she commands, and takes me entirely by surprise.

"Bon—"

"Sit."

I sit. She paces back and forth with her hands curled into fists by her side. Damn, she's quite intimidating. I see the fire in her eyes again, and my ridiculous body lights up. Why do I have to find that type of behaviour so attractive?

After a few more trips back and forth, she stops directly in front of me. "One, I would never kiss you, or anyone, with hate or anger. I'm not built that way and I'm mad at you for thinking I would be capable of doing that. We might have a lot to learn about each other, but I'd like to think you know me well enough to never think I'd do such a thing."

I go to respond, but she flicks my nose, which stuns me. No one has ever *flicked* my fucking nose to get me to shut up. It makes me want to laugh.

"Second... I still want to kiss you. And third, I really like your hair down, but that's just an observation I wanted to voice."

I can't stop from laughing now. She scowls, but stops the second I reach for her hips and draw her to me. We're a reversed version of the kitchen scene and that's fine. I enjoy looking up and into her eyes.

"I want to kiss you, too."

"So do it already." Wow, she's kinda bossy when she wants to be.

Curling my hand around her neck, I pull her down until her lips are a millimetre from touching mine. I just need a second to compose myself because this is a lot to take in, and let's be clear: We're in my bedroom and once I kiss her, I'm not going to stop until I've tasted every inch.

Her tongue breaches my lips, and it's on. We crash together with ragged breaths. My hands travel from her hips to her arse, which makes her buck forward. I pull a little harder until she climbs aboard and straddles my hips. Bonnie takes my hair in her fists again and pulls, earning another moan from me.

I wish to God we weren't wearing so many clothes because I can't wait to get my hands on her. Bonnie must read my thoughts because she instantly starts unbuttoning my blouse. Gone are the nervous fingers she'd displayed when at my door. This Bonnie is fully in charge; another fact that is foreign to me. In the boardroom and bedroom, I'm always the top dog—until now.

Warm air caresses my body as the shirt slips from my shoulders. I suck on her bottom lip as she works on my bra clasp. In seconds, I'm nude from the waist up and having my nipples pinched. My body is on tenterhooks as she trails her fingers down my stomach to the fastener on my pants.

"Lay down," she commands again. I do as I'm told and watch her pull at my trousers. She has me laid bare before her and I start to feel uneasy. That doubt creeps into my mind. Why isn't she naked? Is this a set-up?

Something in my face must relay my feelings because she starts to slowly take off her clothes. Her eyes never leave mine.

"Move up," she whispers. I shuffle up the bed, watching her disrobe. I knew she was hiding an amazing body under all that wool. My God, her breasts are heaven-sent, I swear it.

It's usually around this time when I take over, but I can't. I'm too excited to see what she does with me...*to* me. The last thing she does is release her dark hair from its usual low ponytail. Her Italian roots are shining through as she stands there, watching me watch her. I'm about to ask her what she wants, when the bed dips and she crawls up along my body until she's hovering above me. I can't fucking breathe.

For the first time since she kissed me, I see a sliver of uncertainty. Is she changing her mind?

"I...I'm not very experienced," she murmurs, and oh, thank God, she's not about to hop off and run away.

Taking her hips in my hands again, I lower her to me. Her arousal coats my lower abs. "Do what you want, Bonnie. I'm yours to command."

The fire reignites, and I could cry out in joy as she rocks her hips. Hands planted firmly on either side of my head, she leans down but doesn't kiss me. Instead, she picks up her pace and pants into my mouth. It's possibly the sexiest thing I've ever seen.

My need grows exponentially as she takes her pleasure from riding my body. The pulsing between my legs intensifies as she gets faster and her breath becomes more irregular.

"Look at me," I say, because if she's about to orgasm for the first time, I want to witness every second through her eyes.

Just as I think she's about to come, she stops. I don't have time to question her because she moves up my body until her wetness is dripping over my mouth. My hands brush up her sides until I have her tits in my palms. People who say anything more than a handful is a waste, are fucking morons!

Bonnie's breasts spill out from my hands, but I keep palming them until she sinks her hips to my waiting tongue. Bracing herself against the wall, she begins her assault. I'm still not in charge as she rides my face. All I can do is enjoy the ride and hope she buys a second ticket, because one go is not going to be enough.

I gather her liquid on my tongue and swallow. Her clit pulses with an urgent need to be sucked. The moment I wrap my lips around it, she bucks harder and fills the silence with her growing moans and curses. My name has never sounded so good as it does right now, slipping from her mouth in a gasping plea.

I circle and then suck, repeating until she's quivering and pulling my hair so my face gets even closer. I may not be able to breathe, but, by God, I'm going to shatter her world in the right way. I'm going to make her come so hard she'll be walking on jellied legs for a week.

Just as I think she's finally going to tip over the edge, Bonnie reaches back and swipes her fingers through me. I'm so surprised and turned on I almost choke on her as a deep moan reverberates out of my throat.

Undeterred by my reaction, Bonnie coats her fingers in my pleasure and enters me with force. I'm lighting up from the inside and on the verge of climaxing. Bonnie's renewed thrusts on my face are the only reason I'm able to hold on.

"I'm so close," she gasps, and all I can do is suck her harder. She fucks me with precision and determination until my thighs shake violently and there isn't a thing I can do to stop the orgasm from hijacking my every cell.

21

Bonnie

"ALLEGRA!" I HEAR MYSELF scream as I flood her face.

I'm partly mortified and partly thrilled. I've never gushed. In fact, I thought it was an urban legend. Kelley thought so too. Well, I've dispelled that belief, alright.

My breathing is somewhere between an asthmatic bear and a mewling kitten pleading for air. My skin feels alive and my brain is buzzing. I can't even describe what's happening in my nether regions.

Allegra taps my thigh and I gasp, because I'm sure I've nearly suffocated her if the gulp of air she's taking is anything to go by. I scramble backwards, only to flop forwards on her chest when my hips settle on her upper thighs. My bones are jelly.

Seconds pass and I'm no closer to regulating my heartbeat or air consumption. Allegra doesn't seem to care, though, because I'm suddenly flipped on my back.

"That was fantastic," she says through deep breaths. "I want to do it again."

Well, who the hell am I to say no to that?

"Do you like strap-ons?"

My face flushes before I can cover it up. She pulls at my hands as I try in vain to hide myself. I'm so inexperienced it's embarrassing. What just happened between us is the most daring sex I've ever had.

"I've never tried," I finally blurt out. Her smile makes everything worse. I don't want her pity.

"Hey, we all have to start somewhere, and I quite like the idea of being your first."

Okay, maybe it's not pity.

She sweeps hair from my face, and her eyes soften. "We don't have to use toys if it makes you uncomfortable, Bonnie. I want you to enjoy this as much as me."

Knowing she's enjoying herself spurs me on. I shake my head. "I'm not uncomfortable. I just don't want to disappoint you."

And there I go again, opening my mouth and letting my feelings tumble out without thinking. We've just had incredibly passionate sex and I'm murdering it with my silly hang ups.

"I don't think it's possible," she says quietly. I can't read the emotions scrolling across her face.

"Then I want to try."

Leaning down, Allegra kisses me soft and slow. It's nothing like the lust-fuelled one from moments before. This is deeper and pulls at my heart. Ridiculous, I know. I'm such a fucking cliché.

Pulling away, she chuckles at my sad little whimper. I was no way near ready for the kiss to end. I watch her magnificent backside walk over to a set of double doors. I can see from my position on the bed, she's entered an impressive walk-in wardrobe, that I'm positive holds tens of thousands of pounds worth of Italian clothes.

Allegra, standing with a Ferrari-red dildo in one hand and a leather harness in the other, stops my thoughts about clothing in an instant.

"It's new," she says. I hadn't even thought about that. This is all so overwhelmingly exciting. I don't think I can formulate words. "Do you still want to try?"

I nod my head rapidly, because even though I'm mute, I need her to know I entirely and enthusiastically consent to whatever she wants to do with it. Her eyes light up and a smile graces her lips. She makes a show of slipping the harness on and up her legs. My eyes linger on the patch of darker blonde hair between her thighs. I make a mental note to study that further, later on.

Next, she trails the tip of the dildo between her boobs and down her very sculpted abs. I momentarily panic because I'm in no way sculpted; a little doughy in places, truth be told.

My panic subsides when I see the heat in her gaze. Her blue and green eyes blaze a scorching trail up my body as she places the dildo through the O-ring and begins rubbing the shaft.

Jesus, Mary, and Joseph!

"Would you like to know my favourite way of using this?" she says in a low and dangerous voice.

"Missionary?" I squeak, causing her to laugh deeply.

"No, not quite. I like reverse cowgirl. You know it?"

Oh, bloody hell, there goes my face again. I look away and shake my head.

"Good, I can't wait to show you," she says, stepping forward. "On your knees, Bonnie."

I peel myself off the damp sheets and get to my knees. Allegra circles the bed until she's behind me.

"I'm going to lay down and I want you to straddle my thighs, okay?"

"Okay." I sound breathy, and I know I'm close to hyperventilating.

With a bit of clumsy manoeuvring on my part, I balance myself over her. The tip of the toy pokes my inner thigh, and I'm sure I can feel myself dripping down my leg. This is all highly irregular for me.

"I'm going to rub you all over the toy. Is that okay?"

Is it okay? Um, yes, please. I don't say that, though, because I'm still incapable of saying more than one word, so she gets my nod of the head.

One hand rubs up my back and I shiver. My back is a major erogenous zone for me. Her nails scrape gently as her other hand directs the dildo through my ever-increasing wetness.

"Mmm, you're ready," she says, almost to herself. I love the reverence in her voice.

The hand which was scratching up and down my back now clamps on my shoulder. She raises her hips and pushes the toy into me. I wasn't expecting it to feel so good. I never really got excited over penetration before. But this feels different...or maybe it's who I'm with that is the deciding factor.

"Still okay?" she asks.

"Y-yes," I manage to gasp out.

"You're taking it so well, Bonnie. All my inches."

"Oh, fuck," I cry, because the dirty talk, added to the feeling of her toy inside of me, is revving me up higher than a grandma behind the wheel of a Ford Fiesta.

"Mmm, that's it, relax. Do you want to move your hips?"

Bracing my knees, I lift slightly and roll my hips. It feels amazing, so I do it again. Allegra's hand on my shoulder grips a little hard. When I rise again, her hand pulls me down even harder, and I can't stop the pant and curse slipping from my lips.

"Harder," I say, surprising myself. Allegra doesn't disappoint. She slams into me again and again until I have to hold her legs to keep me steady.

With a sudden move, she sits up behind me and cups both my breasts. "Take what you need from me," she growls.

I feel her stiff nipples rub against my sensitive back. My hips take on a life of their own. I roll deeply, flexing my legs as I rise and fall on her, over and over again. Every time I pound myself against her, she curses and pinches my nipples. I feel her teeth scrape against my neck. I don't think this could get better. And then it does. One of Allegra's hands drops from my breast. I'm too lost in my euphoria to question why she's not playing with my nipple any longer. But my unasked question is answered when I hear a click and the toy starts vibrating, almost making me shoot off her in both surprise and sheer pleasure.

"Oh...oh, yes. Shit, that's... Right there, Allegra."

"Fuck," she says into my neck. We're moving together and it's so damn good. Taking my hands from her legs, I reach back and roughly grab fistfuls of her hair. I'm so wet I'm scared she'll slip out of me before I tumble, but Allegra holds on tighter until I howl through the best orgasm I have ever had.

We fall to the side in exhaustion, Allegra still buried inside of me. "I...I think I like strap-ons," I say, laughing.

Allegra's body shakes behind me. "I'd agree. Hold still."

She turns it off and slips out of me, then removes the harness. I'm slipping into sleep when it occurs to me, Allegra might want me to leave. As upsetting as that would be, I wouldn't argue. Before I can turn to ask, I'm enveloped in her arms as she snuggles behind me, her mouth nestled behind my ear. I lay there and wait for her to say something, but I only hear soft snores. She's already asleep.

Time ticks by. I can't shut off my brain. It's not even the fact we had sex that is keeping me awake; it was the quality. I mean, I thought I'd had great sex before, but now I know it was mediocre at best. How fucking sad. And yet, I'm secretly pleased my earth-shattering orgasms were the result of a night with Allegra Malgeri, mob queen.

I roll my lips to stop myself from laughing, but it doesn't work. Allegra shifts behind me and I feel her head poke over my shoulder.

"Are you laughing?" she asks, which just makes it worse. I'm one of those people that laughs at inappropriate times and once I start, I can't stop.

Allegra simply watches me as I fall about, cackling. I can feel her smile against my skin. When I finally get a grip on myself, I roll until I'm on my back and she's looking down at me.

"Sorry about that," I wheeze.

She grins. "I'm not sure if I should be offended that you find this so funny."

Shaking my head, I bop her on the nose. "That's not what I was laughing about."

"Care to tell me what you found so amusing?"

I nibble my lip. "Okay, but you can't laugh."

"Why not? You did!"

"No, I mean you can't laugh at me."

She brushes her nose against mine...and I melt. "I promise. Now tell me."

"Okay, so before we met—" That's a better way to describe it than *before you abducted me*, which could potentially ruin our very nice evening together. "—I was reading a new book called *Mob's Seduction*."

"That's an appalling title," she scoffs.

"Agreed, but not the point."

"Sorry, continue."

"Well, as you can probably tell, it was about a mob family."

"Shocking," she deadpans. I swat her bottom.

"Anyway. One of the main characters is forced to marry a mob queen to save her family."

Allegra's smile blossoms before me, and she laughs. "Ah, it makes sense now."

"What does?"

"The reason you drunkenly told me you wouldn't marry me and be my sex slave."

Oh shit, yeah. I forgot about that.

"Well, yes. I've been thinking about the book ever since I met you. And..."

"And?"

"And I promised myself I wouldn't fall for your tricks like the main character in the book. But here I am," I grin, "I fell into bed with the mob queen."

She gasps, "So, you are my sex slave!"

"No," I laugh. "Well, maybe. If that's the level of performance I can expect every time."

She scoffs, "Please. That wasn't even my best work."

"I think your best work would kill me, then."

She drops her head to my arm and rubs her nose up and down. I can see she's got something on her mind, so I wait.

"Are...are you okay with what happened? I mean, the part where you slept with someone you vowed not to?"

Running my hand through her hair, I pull a little, so she has to look at me. "I am. I wouldn't have done it if I didn't want to."

She nods. "I know that, but... Well, are you going to regret this later? We've only just started working through some things you find problematic about my life."

Yeah, that's true and I know I'll need more time to really dial into my feelings about it all.

"I won't lie and say it's instantly okay. There's too much going on for me to know how I will eventually feel about everything that's happened. But I know I won't regret this, Allegra. Will you?" This works both ways, after all.

She shakes her head. "No regrets. I'm surprised it happened at all, but I wanted you. I want you."

"Then let's stop talking."

22

Allegra

WE FOUND EACH OTHER again after falling asleep. It was slow, and lazy, and perfect. I honestly thought Bonnie would wake up and freak out, but she didn't. She rolled over, and the dance began again.

Once we'd finished, we didn't go back to sleep. Instead, we spent a few hours talking about everything and nothing. It was refreshing to have a normal conversation that wasn't laced with familial worries or complicated business deals. No matter how hard I try to distance the family from the underworld around us, there is always something lingering in the background, ready to pull me back in.

But last night and the early hours of this morning were different. I didn't have the prickle at the back of my neck as we talked about favourite movies or Bonnie's wool obsession. I had to know where it came from. She took my jibes as they were intended: light-heartedly. I managed to get her to admit she enjoys fine Italian clothing better than a carcigan, so I call that a win.

I found out her favourite colour—orange—which surprised me due to her love of beige wool. Her favourite food? Cheese and onion sausage rolls, and her favourite animal is the Giant Panda. Solid choice; the creatures are cute. Most importantly, I now know her favourite books, which then led me to download *Mob's Seduction*. We read some parts together until we reached the spot Bonnie had reached the day I took her. She refused to read any more and banned me also, which I found funny. She lasted ten minutes until her curiosity got the best of her and we continued the story.

The conversation then took a more serious turn. Bonnie wanted to know more about the other Mafiosi families and our pact. I shouldn't have told her anything, but if anyone deserves some clarity, it's her. She asked about the Arellos and if I really thought she was in as much danger as we originally believed. I understood her confusion, considering Giani hasn't made a move at all. He's quiet—too quiet—and I know that means he's scheming, but I didn't want to freak Bonnie out, so I told her we just needed to be cautious a little while longer until I was sure she could go home.

We both grew quiet when I said "home" because it burst our bubble. As wonderful as our time together has been, it will end. She will go home and resume her life, as I will. Instead of ending things on a down note, I rolled her over and peppered her with kisses. We fell asleep an hour later, after a few more rounds.

The sun kissing the top of my head woke me. I often sleep with the drapes open because I love the smell of the ocean and the breeze, which smells of vines and sea salt. Now I wish I'd shut them so the light hadn't woken me. Because as soon as Bonnie wakes up, it's over.

Maybe one night was all we were ever meant to be. Let's be realistic; we're completely incompatible. Our lives are too different, Bonnie is too innocent, and I hate that she's been dragged into this life through no fault of her own.

She stirs beneath me. I'm wrapped around her with my face against her shoulder. I think it might be my new favourite place. I hardly recognise myself. Days ago, the feelings I had towards Bonnie bordered on contempt, but now I think I got it wrong. I think my heart knew she was dangerous for me and acted accordingly. The anger and frustration were a protective shroud my heart cast around me to prevent this.

One night with Bonnie Moorside and I'm wrecked.

"Mornin'," she mumbles as she turns into me. Her head tucks under my chin as she wiggles her body, burrowing into me. I can't help the smile that forms on my face.

"Good morning," I reply, kissing the top of her head.

"I love your accent," she says sleepily.

"I know. You told me several times last night," I chuckle.

"Well, it's sexy."

"Mmm." I don't want this to end, but a look at my clock tells me it's going to, and fast. I have a lot on my plate and can't shirk off. Bonnie told me she plans to talk to Lorenzo today, and I don't want her to back out of that because she's with me. It's important they get the chance to connect, or at least get some closure.

"Would you like some breakfast?"

"I don't want to move," she mumbles.

"You don't have to," I laugh. Reaching over, I take the phone and dial 1. It's a direct line to the kitchen. With breakfast ordered, I snuggle back down and hold Bonnie for a little while longer. Only when I hear the knock on my bedroom door do I pull myself out of her embrace.

We sit and eat, sipping coffee that makes Bonnie wince. She's never had a proper espresso before, which is a tragedy. I have to explain why Starbucks and Costa Coffee are not the bar to which one compares a good cup of coffee.

"I have to go to the office," I say once the food is finished and coffee is drunk. I can't put it off any longer. She nods, but doesn't look at me. "Bonnie?"

Sucking in a breath, she lifts her eyes. "Is this it?"

What can I say? I don't want it to be a one-night stand, but in what universe could we ever be more? There is already a ticking clock counting down to the day she leaves Italy.

"I think it has to be," I say softly. "I think a friendship with you is all I can ask. If you want that, too."

She smiles gently and cups my cheek. "It's not what I want, but I don't think we have any other choice."

I close my eyes because looking into her face is causing me actual pain. She's so beautiful, and I'm angry at myself for allowing this to happen. As wonderful as it has been, I've well and truly set myself up for pain, just like I did with Petra. Only this will be worse, because I know Bonnie is a good person. She's nothing like Petra, and in another life where I'm not on the cusp of becoming Donna Malgeri, I would have held on to Bonnie and never let her go, because she is the real deal.

We dress and Bonnie leaves with a sweet kiss on the cheek. I'm sure, like me, she will take a bit of time to fully digest what happened between us. But I'll have to do my processing later. I've got work to do.

"So, you fucked her then," Rosa says from my office door. I clench my jaw and pretend her casual use of the word "fuck" is anything but an insult to what Bonnie and I did last night.

"Careful, Rosa," I caution.

I don't have to see the eyeroll to know she's doing it. Pushing off the frame, Rosa settles in the chair opposite me. "No need to get sensitive. I'm just a bit surprised."

"As was I."

"Good, though?"

"Fantastic," I murmur.

"And this morning?"

I shrug. "It didn't end in tears, if that's what you mean."

"Okay. Good talk. Now, on to business. Giani is way too quiet. His absence isn't sitting right with me, Allegra."

Putting my pen down, I lean back and look up, closing my eyes. Just one day of peace is all I ask.

"I agree, but until he does something, my hands are tied. The other families are aware of the situation. I can't undermine the pact, otherwise Giani wins. I need him to fuck up first."

Rosa rubs her chin. "Shall I double the surveillance, then?"

"Yes. I want to know where he is at all times."

"Done. Are you personally receiving this week's shipment?"

Nodding, I stretch my neck. "Yes, I'll head to the docks tomorrow night. Changing up the schedule was a good idea. It stops the Arellos from fucking with any more of our cargo. I don't know if I can talk Lorenzo down if it happens again."

Rosa bites her lip. "Are you going to tell him you want out?" she says. I freeze at the prospect.

Is that what I want? To be fully out and free of the mob? The thought would have been unthinkable a few months ago. So much has changed.

"Meaning?" I ask.

She shrugs. "I'm not stupid, Allegra. For all your blustering about becoming Donna Malgeri, you're miserable. And don't think I haven't noticed the decrease in shipments recently. You're slowly pulling the family away from that side of things. You have been since taking the lead."

I smile at her because Rosa always impresses me. She's smart and on the ball. Putting aside her mistake the other night, Rosa is the ultimate professional and is keen to learn.

"Is that a problem for you?" There are people in this life who love it. I'm talking about the criminal aspect; they love the rush and some enjoy the cruelty. Giani Arello is a prime example.

"No, why would it be? As long as we're making money, I don't give a shit either way. I'm just worried."

"About?"

"Lorenzo. As much as he's tried to steer the family in the right direction, he's still his father's son. The Ferrante family is at the top of the food chain, and I'm worried he won't be as happy to leave that part of things behind. It's in his blood, Allegra."

"It's in mine too. Trust me, I understand. The money we make through that line of revenue is staggering. It's easy money and it keeps us in power. But is that a good reason to risk our freedom? I'm not being dramatic when I say our lives are in constant danger. We're not untouchable, as much as the other families like to believe. The Ferrante family has more money than God! We don't need any more. But we do need to be smart and make sure we're still around to spend our billions. Every time we secure a shipment, I'm aware it could be our last. For all I know, the feds will be waiting for me tomorrow and I'm tired of living like that when it isn't necessary."

"Hey, I get it. I think the rest of the family will too, as long as they get to keep their lifestyles. But Lorenzo?"

"He will see sense. He has to. Maybe Bonnie's appearance is the key."

"Maybe. Just tread carefully, Allegra. You're not the named Donna of this house just yet."

"I understand. And thank you, Rosa. I don't know what I would do without you."

Our impromptu conversation has a pit of vipers curling around my stomach. I feel like I'm battling on all sides right now. Surely Lorenzo won't fight me on this? Not when he's already so tired and ready to retire. He has to see there is no future for the family if we stay on this road. One day the Mafiosi will be taken out, and I don't want us anywhere near it when it happens.

I need some air. The Arellos, Lorenzo, and the shipment tomorrow, follow me like a black cloud. I'd like to tick one thing off my list so it isn't weighing me down. The shipment tomorrow is the only thing I can really control right now. I'll reach out to our guy inside the feds to make sure we're not on anyone's radar. It's not a surefire way to make sure we're not under surveillance. The law knows we have people in their ranks and are usually extremely guarded about any plans they have against us. Our guy is solid, though. No one would suspect him, so I have faith I can trust him if he tells us everything is quiet.

The sea air fills my lungs and I feel the darkness clear. I may not like doing this job very much, but I'm damn good at it. I'll work out a way to convince Lorenzo we need to permanently step away from the Mafiosi. I'll deal with the Arellos. I'll do it all, because I'm heiress Allegra Malgeri, soon to be named Donna Malgeri of the Ferrante family.

I'll do it, because it's the only way I could possibly have a real chance with Bonnie Moorside.

23

Bonnie

SLEEPING WITH ALLEGRA HAS added a hundred pounds of confusion to my already weighed-down brain cells. But it was so worth it, even with Dad staring at me like I've lost my mind as soon as he spots me coming down the stairs. Ideally, I'd like a few more hours to bask in the afterglow of the best night of my sexual life, to date. Clearly, that's a pipe dream.

"Honey," he begins in a tone I don't like.

"Dad. Good morning."

"Will you sit with me a moment?" It's not really a question.

"Sure." We make our way to the kitchen breakfast bar. My stomach rumbles. Not surprising, really, after the workout Allegra put me through. "I'm going to grab a yoghurt. Do you want anything?"

I'm trying to act as normally as possible, hoping it magically stops the conversation I'm about to have from happening.

"So," he says, letting his word hang there. I'm not going to make it that easy on him. Finishing the yoghurt, I reach for an orange. "Bonnie?"

"Dad?"

He huffs in frustration. "Bonnie, what are you thinking? Didn't we talk about this?"

"Define 'this'," I reply.

"Lorenzo and Allegra. Who they are. Who they will always be."

"We did, and I took on board what you said."

"Really?" He laughs mirthlessly. "Interesting, considering you spent the night with her."

"I did. It's complicated with her. And it was a one-time thing. I listened to you, Dad, but you're forgetting I'm a grown woman who can make her own decisions. And someone who will own their mistakes. Which, for the record, I don't think being with Allegra was."

"She's a career criminal," he stresses.

"I know who she is. Better than you, I'd wager."

"Do you hear yourself? Honey, you slept with a mob boss."

Okay, I'm done with this. "Enough, Dad. You've said your piece, and I've given you my reply. I'm not your patient. I'm your grown daughter, who you raised to be independent. You may not like my choices, but you don't get to sit there and judge me for them."

"I'm not judging you, sweetheart."

"Ha! That's exactly what you're doing. Are you telling me after all the time you've spent talking with Lorenzo, you still only see him as the Don of a Mob family?"

"No, but—"

"But nothing. Lorenzo and Allegra are complicated. Their lives are complicated. I judged them from the beginning, and rightly so, but things have changed. I understand their lives aren't something I want to be a part of. Allegra knows that, which is why it was a one-night deal. And something I shouldn't have to explain to you, because it's none of your business, Dad."

"You're my little girl, Bonnie."

"I'm your adult daughter. Trust me."

"Phillip?" Pop says from the doorway. "What's going on?"

Ah, it makes sense now why Dad is the only one giving me a lecture. Pop didn't know he was going to do it. "Mark, I was just—"

"Doing the very thing we decided not to do last night," Pop says.

"Hey, I don't want you two arguing," I interrupt. "Dad knows where I stand, and that's where I want to leave it, okay? I've got another important conversation to get through today, and I'll probably need you both later to wade through the emotions it's sure to mix up."

"You got it, pumpkin. Lorenzo is a good man, despite what some people think." Oh, Pop has his snarky pants on. I feel sorry for Dad. He's in the doghouse for a few days, for sure.

I'm not lying. The talk with Lorenzo is firmly at the forefront of my mind now. Allegra is still there, too, however, she's less of an unknown now. Lorenzo is still a stranger; a man that makes up half of me that I know nothing about. Now the shock has worn off, I know I'm ready to learn about that part of my family.

Before I speak to him, though, I need a nap. I'm seriously sleep deprived.

"Where the hell did you get to last night, lady?" Pete sashays in and stops dramatically with both hands on the breakfast bar. Dad and Pops give a small smile and leave, which is probably wise.

"Hello, Pete," I say, ignoring his question. Kelley comes rushing in, her hair a hive of chaos.

"Oh, no, where were you, Bonnie Moorside?" he asks.

"Yeah, Bonnie, where were you?" Kelley chuckles, waggling her eyebrows.

"Stop it," I say, going red.

"Nuh-uh. You got freaky with the Ice Bitch, didn't you?" Pete says with a gasp.

"Don't call her that," I snap and then wince.

"Ooh, she's protective. Damn, Bonnie, put the claws away," he cackles.

"Did you really sleep with her?" Kelley asks. Shit, is she mad? She'd have every reason to be. After all, she's the one that has been hurt the most in all this.

"I did." I'm always honest with Kelley, so I'll deal with whatever she has to say—more so than I did with Dad.

She nods her head slowly. "I slept with Beth," she squeaks. My mouth pops open in surprise.

"Jesus," Pete gasps, "it's like a hotbed of lesbian mafia love all up in here!"

"Okay, okay, we need a pizza night!" I declare. "Tonight. My room at eight. I need to take a nap and talk to Lorenzo, then we'll debrief over delicious carbs."

"Now, that's a plan I can get behind," Pete says, clapping his hands. "Okay team, hands in." Kelley and I put our hands on Pete's, giggling. This is so silly, but just what I need. "In three," he calls. "One. Two. Three... Mafia lesbians are hot," he shouts enthusiastically. I roll my eyes, and Kelley nods her head in agreement.

I fall asleep as soon as my head hits the pillow. I dream vividly and wake up feeling flushed. Crikey, is this what I can expect from now on? Sex-fuelled dreams that leave me feeling wired every morning? God, I hope so. It beats waking up with anxiety sweats.

I shower and dress carefully. It's not a job interview but feels as important. Lorenzo is in the restaurant waiting for me, and I'm sure he's just as nervous as I am. The thought makes me wonder if I do anything similar to him behaviour-wise when I'm nervous. Does he pace or tap his chin? I do, and I didn't get it from my dads. These types of thoughts have been popping up regularly over the past few days.

He's sitting at a table near the newly installed bar, but he isn't drinking wine. He's tapping his finger on the side of a frosted glass of water whilst staring into space.

"Um, hi," I say quietly.

He startles, but pulls it together quickly. The smile on his face is genuine, and once again it's a little disconcerting seeing myself in him.

"Bonnie, hi. Please, sit. Water?"

"Please."

He skips to the bar. I watch him grab a fresh bottle of sparkling water out of the fridge. Instead of passing me the bottle, he goes to the trouble of pouring it into a glass with ice and a slice of lemon. It's a stalling tactic, and that's okay.

"Here you go," he says. Instead of sitting back down, he shuffles on the spot for a second, looking entirely uncomfortable, until I raise my eyebrow and he sits his bum down with a smile. "I'm sorry, I'm quite nervous," he admits.

"Me too. But I think that's normal."

"You look like her, you know. Maria."

"Have you got a picture?"

Reaching around to his back pocket, Lorenzo opens his wallet and rifles around for a second. He produces a small photo that makes him smile, but I also see the sadness. I think he really did love my mother, and that's just tragic. A potential family was torn apart because of...what? Mob politics and jealousy? It makes me so angry.

"Here."

Taking the picture, I take a steadying breath before letting my eyes drop. I may have Lorenzo's hair and eye colour, but wow, everything else about me is all Maria. She was gorgeous.

"Gosh."

"She was the best woman I ever knew. It broke my heart to send her away. If you believe anything, please believe that."

Tears sting my eyes. "Why didn't you do more?" I croak.

"Because I was scared, Bonnie. This life has taken everything from me."

"And yet you haven't learned your lesson," I snap.

"You're right. But once you were gone, I had nothing good left in my life, until Allegra."

"But... Why didn't you come for me when your wife died?"

Lorenzo looks at the table, lost in his mind and memories. I let my tears fall. I think it's the healthiest breakdown I've had for a while.

"What could I give you, Bonnie? Your dads were raising you in a loving home, far from violence. I wanted that for you. Hell, I wanted it for Allegra, but this life is all I had to offer. Walking away meant leaving with nothing. No legacy."

That's what it comes down to? Legacy? I shake my head. "Legacy. That's..."

"Selfish and unimportant?"

"Yes. Both."

"You're right, of course. But I can't take back my decisions, Bonnie. God knows I wish I could. I'd do anything to have your mother by my side. I dreamed of the life we would have had as a family."

"What was she like?"

"Kind and intelligent. She had this light that shone on you whenever she cast her gaze your way. I fell in love with her the second our eyes met. She was a gifted artist and avid reader."

"Was she... Did she come from one of the families?"

"No," he says, shaking his head. "Her family were farmers. They were our neighbours for a long time. But we ran in different circles, which is why I didn't meet her until I was older and already married. Maria had just taken over from her mother, delivering food. We had a big family event on, and our chef only bought fresh ingredients from Maria's family farm. They were the best. I wanted to check on the food and happened to run into her—literally. I tried to juggle the vegetables I'd knocked from her hand, but I ended up making it all worse," he laughs, "and that was it. She fell for me just as hard, but it was impossible. We tried to stay away from each other for a long time. I had a wife, and Maria was supposed to marry another man."

"Giani Arello?"

"Yes. But it wasn't love. Maria felt forced into it. How could she say no to an Arello? Our attempts to stay away from one another failed. The connection was too strong, and I knew it was true love. Sappy, right?"

"Romantic. Sad, too, but not sappy."

"She wanted me to run away with her. But I couldn't. We would never have found peace. When she told me she was pregnant, my first thought was getting her and the baby out of Sicily. She was crushed, and I'll never forgive myself for putting that look on her face. And for failing her, and you, so spectacularly. I think that's why I didn't come for you, Bonnie. I wasn't worthy."

"I can't say it's not hard to hear," I begin. "Until last week, I didn't give you a thought. My dads did a great job, even if Allegra thinks my love of wool garments would say otherwise. Maybe it would have been different if my life hadn't gone the way it had."

"Allegra was my second chance," he admits. "She needed me, and her parents were already in the family. I could parent her how I'd been parented. It might seem like I forced her into this life, and I suppose you're right to think that, but I believe with my whole heart she was better here with me than being taken to an orphanage."

"Your relationship with Allegra is none of my business." I can't think of her right now.

"She's not a monster, Bonnie."

"I know." My heart skips a beat. She's no monster, but she's no angel, either.

24

Allegra

WAKING UP WRAPPED AROUND Bonnie seems like a lifetime ago, even though, in reality it's been, roughly, only fourteen hours. My day is one long drag as I try to make it to the other end with my sanity in one piece.

I could be exaggerating. The docks always leave me feeling wound up. It's the stress of never really knowing if I'm being set up, or if our contacts will suddenly want to renegotiate their contract and rates, or if the cargo is damaged or incorrect. There is nothing about visiting the docks that makes me happy, especially tonight when I had to deal with a newbie.

The only thing that got me through the ordeal was the thought of a glass of wine and my balcony. Bonnie zipped through my mind, but I shut that down. I can't afford to want her. Last night and this morning were perfect—too perfect. We met under extreme circumstances and emotions have been high from day one. My mind refuses to let my soft heart think there could be anything real with her, even though this morning I still had a glimmer of hope, I now know it's foolish.

When the dust settles, and Bonnie is back home, this will all be just a memory to her. Actually, I think that's when she'll come to understand she made a mistake. It hurts to think that, but it's true. When her nerves and emotions are not calling the shots, she'll be glad she got away from me. That's why I focus on the bottle of wine instead of the woman who surprises me at every turn.

The villa is dark by the time I return home. I make a quick snack board and trudge upstairs. I can't wait to let my hair down—literally. When I no longer have to present myself as the Ice Bitch, I think I'll make a point of always leaving my hair down. No more headaches for me.

I pass Bonnie's door and stop. Giggling and laughter vibrate through the wood, which makes me smile. It sounds like Bonnie, Kelley, and Pete are having a good time. I briefly wonder if she's told them about last night. My ego swells because I know I showed her a good time.

Leaving them to what I can only presume is an adult slumber party, I slip into my room and lean against the door as it closes. A rush of air leaves my lungs as I let my frustration go with the breath. Settling the open bottle of wine on my balcony table, I perform the perfunctory bedtime routine of showering and dressing in silk pyjamas. I'll sleep naked, but there are mosquitos outside and the little bastards love feasting on me.

As usual, the night sky doesn't disappoint. I allow myself several minutes of deep breathing before taking my first sip of wine. I make sure I indulge in every drop. It's the sort of ritual that helps me cast the day away. Listening to the ocean and the crickets, I settle into my seat. My body feels heavy from the stress of the day. There's a sore spot on my lower back where my pistol rubbed through my shirt. I make a mental note to put it in the gun safe as soon as I go inside.

The call from Luke I received earlier in the day plays on my mind. He's a good man and a loyal employee. I feel bad for exploiting his need for extra cash. But that's what I do best, I suppose. A deep sigh leaves my tired body. I wonder if I can really take the Ferrante family out of the Mafiosi and go fully legit.

Isn't being the top of the mob who we are? Can we ever really shed our old life and start anew? The optimistic side of me screams "yes". That's what we can and must do. But the other side that grew up around mobsters and criminals begs to differ. This way of life is ingrained in us. How long would it be until family members became restless and wanted something more? Something that gave them the thrill of old times? I'm a mess of contradictions and it's pissing me off.

Being decisive is my strong suit. Yet right now, I feel so unsure. I've worked my fingers to the bone to make sure the family is set up for life, but that doesn't mean it will work out the way I hope. Lorenzo is still the named head of the house. Until he formally steps aside, I'm living on a wing and a prayer. He could refuse to name me Donna after he learns of my plans to take us out of this life.

Dammit, I'm supposed to be unwinding and all I'm doing is getting myself more wound up with the unknown. Plus, I've gone off on a tangent. Luke's call—that's what I was focusing on. The call informed me Giani was in his bar and acting oddly. Instead of his usual garish and bullish behaviour, Luke told me he was distant and silent as his men drank and got rowdy.

Something is brewing, and I wish it would just fucking happen so I can react and end this. Bonnie, her parents, and her friends are nothing but prisoners here. Anyone can paint it up to look like a holiday in a luxury villa, but the truth is they are incarcerated and unable to leave the proximity of the villa for fear of an attack.

I want this finished—now. But Giani isn't making a move—yet. I wonder if he's waiting to see if I'll grow complacent. He's an opportunist, after all. But then I think of him sitting in Luke's, plotting, because that's exactly what I think he's doing: sitting there silently, combing through ways to get to Bonnie and hurt Lorenzo.

What he doesn't know, though, is he would be hurting me too. I cannot think of her getting hurt without a boiling rage exploding through my veins. Sometimes I wish I could go back to the days where I couldn't wait to get rid of the irritating woman. It would be easier to deal with this if that were the case. When emotions are involved, lines get blurred and mistakes are made.

Tossing back the last of my wine, I plod to the bed more irritated than when I got home. I discard my pyjamas and slide under the sheets. The scent of Bonnie hits me like a truck and my heart squeezes, as does another part of my anatomy. I can't help the way my body reacts.

The sheets will have to be stripped and cleaned first thing in the morning, because this is torture. More deep breathing gets me to a state where I might doze off. The light tapping on my door pulls me from the brink of sleep, and at first, I think I'm hearing things. But then it happens again.

Leaning up on my elbows, I stare at the door, hoping. Could it be?

"Enter," I call. The door creaks open and a low light casts her in shadow. I'd know that silhouette anywhere.

Bonnie remains silent as she gently shuts the door behind her. I watch her with rapt attention, unable to speak lest I ruin the magic of this moment. It's possibly a wonderful dream, and if so, I'd like to live in it a little while longer.

Moonlight drenches my room in a soft blue palette. Bonnie takes a step forward and brings her hands to her top. She unbuttons it slowly, taking her time to read my body language. The skirt is next, and then I'm lying there, looking at her in lace. My breath sits in my throat, refusing to move either way.

I should tell her this is a bad idea, and that last night was perfect; leave it there and hold on to the memory of that—but I can't. I want her again. Drawing the sheet to one side, I open up my bed as an invitation. Bonnie unhooks her bra and slips down her thong.

She slides in, facing me. Her hand comes to my face, cupping my cheek. It's delicate, like this moment. I can smell wine on her breath, but her eyes are clear. She's probably had less than me and I'm no way near drunk.

"One more night," she whispers.

The only answer I can give is with my mouth as it crashes into hers. I'm acting foolish, I know, but I'll suffer the consequences later.

Her body melts into me as I clutch her hips with growing urgency. The fatigue and stress of the day are a distant memory as she gives herself to me. Rolling us over, I hover above, drinking her in. The moonlight casts us in shadow, but her eyes sparkle. If I didn't know better, I'd say we're in the middle of a *Mob's Seduction* love scene. Unlike the characters, though, Bonnie and I can't have the happily ever after. This is just an indulgence we both need to satisfy before we go back to our own worlds.

"Stay with me," she says.

My mind snaps back to her with startling clarity. I have such a finite amount of time with her I refuse to lose a second of it to a wandering mind. My hips lower and roll. We're both wet already; proof of our chemistry. She threads her hands through my hair, just like last night.

"Don't close your eyes," I say.

She bites her lip and stares at me, enough to feel it in my very soul.

We work together, rolling and thrusting. Her breasts rub against me as her body moves. I want to take her nipple in my mouth, but I can't move. Looking down on her as she takes her pleasure is addictive. It's not the most adventurous sex, but *mio Dio*, it feels sublime.

The sounds emanating from our joined bodies are obscene, only adding to the charged tension coiling between us. Sweat forms on my back as I grind and thrust deeper, causing us both to roll our eyes in pleasure. I'm close and Bonnie is too. I know because she's panting hard and her hands grip my arse with a strength I didn't know she possessed.

Her body shakes and her muscles tense. I feel the second she tips over and allow myself to follow blindly as we moan into each other's necks. Pulses of electricity charge through every neuron as I succumb to her. Only when I've depleted every last bit of energy, do I collapse. Her arms snake around me and we lay there, breathing hard.

Aware I'm possibly squashing her, I slip to the side. My leg hitches over hers and my head rests on her shoulder. Should I say something, ask what this was, or just enjoy what I can get?

"Maybe I shouldn't have come in here," she begins. "I know it was selfish, but I couldn't stay away, Allegra."

I like it so much better now she says my name with softness rather than a scathing heat.

"I could have asked you to leave."

"But you didn't."

"I don't think I could have made the words leave my mouth." It's true.

She pulls me closer. "I don't want to talk this to death. I'm tired of talking about everything within an inch of its life. Can we just enjoy each other while I'm here?"

It's such a bad idea. One, or probably both, of us are heading for a world of hurt, but just like before, when she stood in front of me undressing, I am powerless to say no.

"We can do that... if you're sure." No doubt her fathers had something to say about last night. I hope this isn't some silly reaction to their disapproval. That would cheapen what we have.

"I'm sure. I want you, Allegra. For as long as I can."

I nod and kiss the skin above her breast. "Then let's not waste any more time."

If a few nights are all I have, then I'll happily forego sleep to show her what she's come to mean to me.

This mob queen is falling hard. What a shame the landing is going to break me.

25

Bonnie

I'VE ESTABLISHED I'M NOT the risk-taking type of woman. I choose safety and security every time. It's served me well in life, so far. I understand how being inclined that way leads to a more solitary life. Quiet and boring, as Pete would say, but I've always been okay with that. I still am, as a matter of fact. Books and microwave meals might sound pathetic, but as the adage goes: *If it ain't broke, don't fix it.*

There are things I could do a little differently, like upgrade my apartment and wardrobe. I'm starting to see the appeal of different fabrics now. So, there is room for growth, but the fundamental things that make me, *me,* haven't changed, and won't in the future. To risk something is to expose yourself. It makes you vulnerable, and it comes down to the fact that nothing and no one has ever made me want to change the way I operate. No one has made me want to expose myself like that...until Allegra.

Now, I'm not saying I'm suddenly going to become a different person. That's nuts. I'm too anxious and set in my ways for that. But I will dive out of my comfort zone with her—*for* her, if she wants the same thing. I'll do it for the time being, anyway. Maybe it helps knowing there is a time limit on my foray into the unknown that makes the decision easier.

It could have been the extensive talk I had in my room with Kelley and Pete that finally won me over to the dark side. Maybe it's simply that Allegra means more to me than playing it safe, which is crazy considering how we got here. Everything has moved at the speed of light, but I'm not worried, which in itself should probably worry me.

I've learned so much about myself in such a small amount of time. Lorenzo, filling in some missing history, began it all. Our conversation became fraught a few times, but he never backed down. He told me all about my mother, my grandparents on both sides, and my other extended family.

I didn't need it to fill a void or anything. I've never felt like I was missing something. It did open me up to a new side of myself, though; one I never thought to question or explore: the person I could have been given different circumstances. It explained parts of my character that lay hidden, or at least dormant, more often than not, and the fiery side that only pops up now and then. My normal, shy demeanour always wins out until I've had my fill and explode. That side is my mother, apparently. Facial quirks and mannerisms, I inherited from Lorenzo.

I put aside the fact he is a mobster and concentrated on him as a man—a man who loved me and let me go. It's the only way I could see myself comfortably getting to know him. He understood when I explained it to him. It raised the question of how our relationship would grow once I left. We agreed that it had a chance if he were to visit me as Lorenzo Ferrante, dad-wannabe, rather than Don Ferrante, head of a Mafia family. I don't really know how that will work, but it gave both of us hope we could build something. As I've always done, I consulted my dads afterwards and, of course, they gave me their full support.

Pete and Kelley then whisked me away before our meet-up time. Both were too excited to delve into a night of gossip and friendship. Pete plied us with ice cream. We shared one bottle of wine. I listened with utter devotion to Kelley as she told us all about how she and Beth had slept together. Apparently, all the shy looks and lingering touches became too much and they had a passion-filled night of carefully orchestrated sex. Kelley's arm is on the mend, but still not ready for acrobatic debauchery. She blushed through the entire story.

Pete asked if they'd talked about starting anything serious, but Kelley shook her head. She's so like me. I knew her head would win over her libido. Then all eyes turned to me and I told them about my night with Allegra. They listened and poked fun every time I wandered off into a delicious memory.

Pete asked the same question: Were we planning on starting something more serious? He got the same answer Kelley gave. And that's when he offered his opinion. For once, it wasn't about forgetting my worries and getting plastered. He advised seizing the day and enjoying the moment.

My usual rebuff didn't manifest as I sat there listening to him. I wanted more time with Allegra. It wasn't the safest option, not for my heart anyway, but I knew I'd regret it if I didn't at least try. So that's how I found myself at her door, entering her room, and stripping off, praying she wouldn't send me away.

Our bodies came together effortlessly, and I knew as she collapsed onto me, I'd made the right choice. I wanted the unsafe and unsecure just for a little while. And I didn't want to thrash our complicated relationship to death until I changed my mind.

Allegra's willingness to give us that, set a fire between us and we delved in for more hours of sex that left us sated and wrung out. It differed from last night. There were so many unspoken words we could only communicate through touch, that every brush of a fingertip, or ghost of a breath on each other's skin, became something more; something deeper...something that could only exist in that moment.

"Are you still awake?" she asks me in a thick voice. It's partly from the workout her voice box has just gone through and the pull of sleep.

"Yeah, I'm still awake. Just enjoying the moon."

She shifts beside me, so I turn to look at her. The glint of metal on her bedside table catches my eye. It's her gun. The one that put a bullet in Kelley. I can't help the slight hitch in my breath as I look at it. Allegra feels the change in me and turns to look where my eyes are focused. She curses in Italian and extracts herself from me, taking the gun. There are several mechanical clicks and then she's back, her eyes searching my face. I'm sure she's expecting me to rant and rave, or even leave, but I don't.

"I'm sorry. I meant to put it away earlier." Her voice wavers.

What can I say? I know things like that are a part of her daily life. I don't want to judge her. And I won't. But our glorious and unfettered time together is ruined. Maybe it's more like it brings us back to reality. The gun is a stark reminder of why a few nights of sex are all we can have. No matter how much Allegra wants to set the family on a different path, mobsters will always surround the Ferrante family. How could they ever truly separate themselves from a life they've spent so long building?

"Did you need that for your meeting?" I ask. I knew she had business away from the villa, but I didn't ask for specifics.

"Only as a precaution."

She's unsettled, and a little panicked, so I coax her back into my arms. "No problems?"

"No."

We fall silent. I focus on the steady exhale of our breaths. I hate the fact she went somewhere today that could have put her in danger, and I hate the fact that carrying a gun is so natural for her.

"Do you have to go out again tomorrow?"

"No. The seasonal workers are arriving early in the morning. We only have a few days before the harvest begins."

"You sound excited." And I'm happy to move on. Hating that uglier part of her life won't change anything. I'd rather claim ignorance and pretend it doesn't exist.

She rubs her face against my chest and tickles her fingertips across my belly. It brings a smile to my face.

"It's my favourite time of the year. Everyone comes together. It's back breaking, but so gratifying. On the night of the first harvest day, we have a big meal with last year's wine and Mamma Picollo's food."

"Sounds fun. I can't wait to join in...if I'm allowed." It occurs to me the vines are outside my designated safety zone.

"You can stay with me. I'd like to teach you how to pick the grapes if you'd like?"

I scoot down the bed and roll to my side. We're nose-to-nose, and I can't help but place a kiss on the tip. "I would really like that! Can Kelley and Pete help?"

"Of course. Kelley might be better taking an observational role though. Her shoulder needs more rest."

I laugh. "She'll love it. Bossing Pete around will make her so happy."

"You are a strange trio of friends," she grins. "He's so different to you and Kelley."

"He is, but it works. Sometimes you need a bit of something different to balance you out. Know what I mean?"

She pecks my lips. "I know exactly what you mean."

"Plus, he's super loyal and protective. Pete saved me from many a wedgie at school. I don't know why he decided he wanted to be my friend. It's not like we had anything in common back then either. Pete was the strapping sports nut, and I was the mousey book nerd with two dads."

"I bet you were the cutest book nerd at the school," she chuckles.

"Well, obviously," I reply with confidence. "Anyway, he stood up for me and that was that. He does the same for Kelley."

"Maybe I was a bit rash to shout at him then," she murmurs into another slow kiss. Gosh, I could live on them.

"No, you weren't. He needed to hear it, and I think he'd probably thank you if he weren't so petrified."

She sighs. "I don't want him to be petrified of me. He's your friend."

"Then feel free to talk to him. Kelley, too."

"Kelley's a different matter," she says, her eyes cast downward.

"You apologised, and she's moved on. Plus, she's smushing bits with Beth, so her focus is definitely not on you!"

Her eyes grow wide. "She's fucking Beth?"

"Well, one time at least. Not sure if it will happen again."

Allegra grins wolfishly. "*Mob's Seduction* at its finest."

I roll my eyes and bite her lip. "Nonsense. Beth's hot. That's all there is to it."

"You think Beth's hot?"

Oh, the indignation I've noticed anyone apart from her is delicious.

"Yes, have you seen her? I mean, she's got an ass you could bounce a penny off."

"I've got an ass you could do that with, too!"

Keeping a straight face right now is the hardest thing I've ever had to do. "Sure, but Beth has such blue eyes."

"I've got a deep blue eye and an emerald one! Next?"

"Her rack—"

"No way. My tits are amazing. I know you like them," she huffs, and that's it. I crack, cackling into the silence.

"Oh my God, you are ridiculous!"

She furrows her eyebrows and pouts her lips. "I'm not ridiculous," she grumbles.

The cuteness is too much, so I gather her face in my palms and lay the deepest kiss I can on her. It quickly turns hotter than the sun, and I find myself parched for her body.

Allegra must feel the same because no sooner have I thought about it, she's flipping me on my back. She gives me a wink and manoeuvres herself so I'm looking at her gathering wetness. She straddles me so her back is against the headboard. I'm thrilled this is the first time I will experience 69ing.

My legs spasm as she dives in, lapping at me as if my excitement were an oasis in the desert. Not wanting to fumble my first attempt at the new position, I concentrate on holding back my rapidly approaching orgasm to lay some long, hard strokes against her. She bucks forward and moans, spurring me on. It's suddenly become a competition to see who can make the other come first.

Allegra loses. I perform tongue artistry I didn't know I could, and she shatters on me. Liquid covers my chin and nose. The feel of it ignites my own climax and I scream into her.

Totally worth the risk.

26

Allegra

Screaming pierces through the night. My eyes snap open, disorientated. Am I dreaming? The banging on my door indicates I'm fully awake. Bonnie sits up, wide-eyed. I listen as thunderous steps race around the villa.

"Allegra, get up," Rosa screams.

I'm out of the bed in a flash, yanking open the door. Rosa is dressed already. "What's happening?"

"Fire," she pants. "In the western field."

Fuck! Fires are always a threat in the summer. Usually, by the time we get to harvesting, the likelihood of them happening is low. The temperatures dip to a safe level, but this year we've had an unseasonably hot summer. A heat-wave has gripped most of Europe for months.

We've never had a fire before and I'm momentarily stunned. We can't afford to lose the crops. It will devastate our earnings and will take years to recover. One field is manageable but if the fire spreads, we're in trouble.

"Allegra!" Rosa shouts.

"Take whoever you need to fight the fire. I want the surrounding fields doused with as much water as possible to prevent it from spreading. I'll be right there."

Rosa takes off running. Sprinting to my closet, I dress as fast as I can. Bonnie is still looking confused. I forget she can't understand Italian.

"There's a fire. I need to go and help put it out. Stay here, okay."

"Allegra, I can help."

"Please, Bonnie. I can't be worrying about you when I need to focus. Please stay here." My words aren't meant to hurt her, but they are true. My sole focus has to be on the fire, and it would be impossible if I knew Bonnie was close by—close to danger.

"Okay. I'll stay with Kelley and Pete."

"Thank you," I say, kissing her on the lips.

Racing out of my room, I spot Kelley. "She's in there. Get Pete and stick together. Do not come outside. The air will be thick with smoke."

She nods and sets off to my room.

It's organised chaos. We've trained for this. The risk is too high not to have a plan should the worst happen. It's unfortunate the field ablaze is the one furthest from the villa. It takes precious minutes to get there and every second counts.

The air *is* filled with smoke. I jump on a quad bike and rev the throttle. There's an orange glow lighting up the night sky. "Toni, warn the neighbouring farms," I call over the noise of flames and people screaming directives.

He nods and takes his own quad west towards our closest neighbour. Each member of the vineyard team is trained to use the water hoses. I'm happy to see they are already fighting the fire with a precision usually only found in professional firefighters. All around me, water rains down as they try to soak the unaffected fields.

Rosa barks orders like a drill sergeant. Jumping off my quad, I race to the closest hose. I can't see how much of the field is burning, and until the fire is out, I won't know the true extent of the damage.

"We've covered the surrounding acreage with all the stored water," Rosa shouts next to me.

"We're making headway," I call back, nodding to the blaze. It's still roaring, but the constant assault of water is finally dampening the beast. Hope soars we've averted catastrophe.

An uptick of wind slows our progression. The fire dances to the east, and for a heart-stopping moment, I think it's about to skip into the next field, regardless of our efforts.

More people arrive. Several are from neighbouring farms. They've brought mobile water tanks and begin unloading on the still-burning vines. The fire hisses and spits, but it finally dies down. There's a collective cheer as the last flame is extinguished.

Leaning over with my hands on my thighs, I take a second to breathe. It's difficult with the stench of smoke still prominent, but I think I might pass out if I don't get some oxygen in my lungs.

"Keep watering," I order after I'm done with my mini-breakdown. "We can't afford to let it ignite again. I want someone on every corner of this field until we are certain there will be no flare-ups."

Everyone scuttles around me, preparing to keep working. Lorenzo charges up in his silk dressing gown. "Fuck," he curses. "God damn it. Is everyone okay?"

"All safe. No casualties. We can't say that for this section of the land, though."

"After all these years. I can't believe it happened," he says, shaking his head. "You did well to train them, Allegra. This would have been so much worse otherwise."

Yes, it would have.

"I'm going to walk around and see the extent of our losses. Want to come?"

He nods, and we set off through the mud. The ground is a proverbial quagmire. I'm not worried about that, though. The sun will dry it out quickly. That's the worrying part. The weather predicts another week of record-high temperatures.

"We'll need to get the water butts and tanks filled immediately."

"I'll make sure it's done," Lorenzo says. We walk with purpose around the edge of smouldering plants. So much love and work went into this crop. Old vines that produced exquisite grapes are ruined. I feel the prick of tears and berate myself. I can't be seen as a blubbering mess.

"I'd say two-thirds of the crop in this section is gone."

"Lucky."

Rosa jogs up alongside us. "The starting point seems to be over there," she says, pointing to a charred area roughly fifty metres to our right. "A young seasonal worker who turned up a day early was the one who spotted it. He'd come out to get familiar with the layout of the fields."

"We owe him," I reply. "He saved us from disaster."

The three of us wander over and begin scouring the area. The smell is overwhelming.

"Fuck," I hear Rosa growl. She's bending down with her hand outstretched. I watch her brush some soil away and then pick something up. She turns to me and holds out what looks like a cigarette butt.

My blood runs cold. The fire wasn't the result of the weather. Some stupid asshole was smoking near the plants. My team knows they are never to smoke or have open flames near the foliage or surrounding brush. It's just common sense.

Unfortunately, not everyone is blessed with it. I'm betting one of the early seasonal workers sparked up as they wandered around and dropped the butt without thinking.

"Gather all the new staff in the restaurant, now," I seethe. Rosa doesn't reply. She just leaves.

Lorenzo dips his head and sighs. "Idiots," he growls.

I agree, and I'll make sure I find the moron who is responsible. They'll never work on this island again. After confirming everyone is doing what they're supposed to, I hop back on the quad with Lorenzo riding pillion.

The restaurant is buzzing with worried chatter. Faces I've never seen before sit with wide eyes and soot covering every inch of them. Most of these people would never come into contact with the head of a house, let alone two. When I'm out in the field, working, I stick to the people I know, simply because it's a more relaxing environment for me. I don't have to be *the* Allegra Malgeri. I can just be Allegra, picking fruit like everyone else.

"You know who I am," I start. There are a few nodding heads, but most sit stock-still. "I intended to introduce myself tomorrow, along with the new arrivals. Well, you're about to get acquainted with me sooner." My voice is glacial fury. "Tonight, one of you walked the perimeter of this land, smoking."

There's a rumble of noise. "I promise, Ms Malgeri, it was none of us," a strong young woman says confidently. "I've worked with everyone here for years. We travel around as a group, and we have enough experience and sense to never light anything near the plants."

"Clearly someone did," Lorenzo barks. "Our crew has worked this land for generations. None of them would have been so foolish."

Lorenzo doesn't need an introduction. The embroidered LF on his robe is a big enough clue as to who he is.

The young woman isn't unsettled by Lorenzo's ire. "I promise you, sir. It wasn't any of us. I'll stake my life on it."

A dangerous thing to say to a Don. One I don't think she'd say lightly. Something isn't right.

"Bring Rosa to me, please," I call. I don't give a shit who does it. I just need her here because I have a sinking feeling.

"Allegra," Rosa chimes as she steps into the restaurant.

"I need to see the cigarette butt."

She pulls a small bag out of her combat pants' leg pocket and hands it to me. My eyes gravitate to the tiny gold writing which circles the beginning of the white paper just past the butt.

I feel the blood drain from my face. Lorenzo steps up and holds me by the elbow. "Allegra?"

My head snaps to Rosa. "Get Toni and Mia. Now!" I bellow. My voice must have been loud enough for Toni to hear because he bustles in seconds later. Rosa runs out to find Mia. "Toni, I need your back up piece."

He instantly reaches to his back and pulls out a pistol. It's heavier than mine, but it will have to do.

"Allegra, what's wrong?" Lorenzo asks.

I shove the plastic bag in his hands and run out the door. As soon as Lorenzo sees what I saw, he'll understand. Mia and Rosa are running towards me.

"Giani set the fire. We need to get to the villa now." That's all the direction they need. We race to the house, keeping vigilant. There is no sign of life which could mean anything. If Giani were here, I'd expect to be fired upon, but there is nothing.

We approach the main door in a tactical formation. As with the fire, we've trained for these situations, too. I slip in first, silently looking for any movement. When I'm sure there is none, I signal for the others to enter. Directing Rosa and Mia to the ground floor rooms, Toni and I creep up the stairs. We take our time to check each room. Kelley and Pete's bedrooms are empty, which I expected.

What I didn't expect was to find them unconscious on my bedroom floor. Pete has blood coming from his head and Kelley has a nasty gash on her cheek. I want to run to them, but we need to clear the room first. Toni checks the bathroom and signals it's clear.

My heart drops. Bonnie isn't here. Giani has taken her. I promised to keep her safe and I've failed. Again.

Toni drops to his knees and scoops up Kelley. Rosa and Mia join us and set about helping Pete. I'm rooted to the floor, staring at my now empty bed.

Molten rage fills my body from the tips of my toes. He finally crossed the line. Giani has no clue what's coming for him. I will gut him for this, personally. By the time I am finished, the Arellos will be nothing but a stain on my shoe. I'll burn everything Giani loves to the ground.

Taking out my phone, I send a group message. It's only polite to warn the other families of the carnage I'm about to unleash on that man. I return the phone to my pocket and hand Toni's gun back to him.

"Be ready to leave in ten," I say with steel in my voice.

Stripping off my clothes, I shower and change into black combat pants and a T-shirt. Taking my gun from the safe, I insert a full magazine and send the slide forward, taking a moment to verify I have a round in the chamber. Putting the weapon on "safe", I holster it and add an extra magazine to my belt. Things are going to get messy.

I close my eyes and bring Giani to the forefront of my mind.

You wanted a war. You've got one. I'm going to tear your family apart.

27

Bonnie

OH CRAP, OH CRAP, oh crap...

Not a helpful train of thought, but it's the only train in my brain station that generally describes my state of mind. Describing my brain as a train station shows the level I'm at right now. I can't think straight—or at all. The bag over my head blocks all the light, and the stench of old cigarettes is nauseating. Add that to the enormous headache gripping my skull and it's no wonder I can't think of anything other than *Oh Crap!*

Everything happened so fast. One minute I was sitting on the bed with Kelley and Pete, freaking out over the fire, and the next minute the bedroom door was being kicked in. Kelley screamed. Pete jumped off the bed and tried to fight three men off, but got hit. Kelley was ripped off the bed by her hair and I was socked right in the face. Things went black and stayed that way. I only know I'm awake now because of the sound and smell overwhelming me.

They must have shoved me in the back of a van because I'm rolling about with every bump and turn. I can hear a low-pitched voice, presumably giving instructions now and then, but I don't recognise it. Damn, I wish I could speak Italian. Two years of mediocre French at school is the extent of my linguistic abilities. I don't think screaming, *Ciao, Bella* at the top of my lungs will do any good. It's literally the only Italian I know.

My face really flippin' hurts. Oh, God, I hope Kelley and Pete are alright. And my dads! My heart plummets when I think of Allegra. Was the fire a trap or a ruse? Did they hurt her? Does she know I've been taken?

Please find me, Allegra.

I plead to the universe she hears me. If anyone can get me back, it's her. And God help whoever gets in her way.

The van, or big car, slows down. I can feel the road is rough through the tyres. Gravel, maybe? It will be somewhere remote. They always take hostages to an abandoned building or something. In *Mob's Seduction,* it was an old pig farm. The villain had one of his prized pigs placed in a pen. He was known as Benny the Pork, which, along with the book's title, is stupid—but I digress, Benny would torture his victims and then feed them to his pig.

It's times like this I wish I hadn't finished the book. I wouldn't have if Allegra hadn't downloaded it. It was a bad idea, especially when I'm the hostage. Oh, fuck, fuckity, fuck. Giani's going to feed me to his pig or something.

The brakes squeak as we stop. It's not a smooth manoeuvre and I slam into something hard. A voice next to me makes me jump and recoil. I didn't know there was someone here with me. He shouts in Italian and gets a mouthful in return from one of the men in the front.

A door opens, and then I hear the side panel door slide on rusty rails.

Definitely in a van.

I bet it's one of those small panel vans serial killers use. How many bodies have they thrown in the back of this one? The thought makes my tummy roll.

Strong hands grip my shoulders, and with little effort, haul me to the rough ground. The air is thick with heat and I can still smell smoke. They can't have taken me that far then, right?

I strain to hear anything past the pounding in my ears. I hit the gravel hard and knock my head. There's a slapping sound, and the man with the low-pitched voice rages in

Italian. The goon who had me by the shoulders hisses and lets go of me. I think he got the slap.

No sooner do I sit up than I'm dragged to my feet and hiked over a broad shoulder. The pungent smell of expensive cologne makes my eyes sting.

The air changes as we step into what I think is a building. It carries a musty smell, reminiscent of a room that hasn't been aired out in a long time. I'm jostled and dumped into a soft chair. If my arms weren't tied behind my back, the chair would be quite comfortable.

More shuffling and murmurs, and then it goes silent. Even though I'm blinded by the sack still rammed over my head, I close my eyes and take a deep breath, trying to get myself into a state of calm. I will not let these arseholes know they've scared me. Been there, done that this month.

"Do you know who I am?" the low-pitched voice asks. His English is broken but clear.

"Giani Arello," I reply. Maybe I should play dumb, and pretend I have no idea who he is or why they could have possibly taken me. But then I think of the bloody book again, and remember the character who did that and how it didn't go too well for her. So, I'll do the opposite and hope for the best.

"Ah, so Daddy warned you, huh?"

"If you mean Lorenzo, then no. It was Allegra." I want to warn him she'll come for me and when she does, he's in big trouble, but that would be stupid. I'm sure he's well aware of the shit Allegra is about to bring.

"Yes, Allegra. She's too clever for her own good, at times."

"I think you'll find she's cleverer than you, Mr Arello." Ah, my snarky side is coming out to play.

Great timing as ever, Bonnie!

"She is a child, and this doesn't concern her," he growls.

My mouth runs away with itself as usual. "I'm part of the family. You've just made it her business."

"You're Lorenzo's bastard, not a Ferrante."

"Totally agree," I say. "But the Ferrantes don't seem to make those kinds of distinctions."

The sack over my head is pulled off, along with several strands of my hair. Just what I need, a bald patch to go along with my mangled face.

My hands are untied, which gives a little comfort. I get my first look at Giani Arello and what I see is…huh, unexpected. He's short, probably around my height, and he's round. When I say "round", I'm saying his circumference is impressive and defies physics. His hair is thin and combed back with enough gel to withstand several rounds in a wind tunnel. There's a chemical shimmer hovering over his skin, which I presume is cologne. These guys are wearing it at dangerous levels. It must affect their oxygen intake. Everything about him screams "sleazebag".

He looks at me with a set of bloodshot marbles for eyes. I'd guess he's had a few drinks. "Why aren't you...scared?"

I'm sure he was expecting me to be hysterical, and if this had been a few weeks ago, you bet your bottom I would have been. I'd have hyperventilated in the first ten minutes of my abduction and passed out. But I'm not the same person now. I'm nowhere near the level of calm someone like Allegra would be in this situation, but I'm confident enough she will keep her promise and get me home, so there's no need to have a full meltdown just yet.

"Should I be scared? Are you planning on hurting me?" I can't just rely on Allegra finding me. I need to work this guy and buy some time.

He grins like a classic movie villain. "I'm going to hurt you. That's a promise. I just need Lorenzo here to see it."

Okay, I wasn't expecting him to be that blunt. Time to channel my parents. "I'm nothing to him, Mr Arello. You must know that?"

"He wouldn't have hidden you if that were the case, my dear. No, no. Lorenzo loves you, which is why it will break him when I take you away. Vengeance will be mine."

Time to change tactics. I shake my head and give him the best pitying look I can forge. "I feel bad for you, Mr Arello. You've carried all this anger around for so long. And for what? Don't you get it?"

"Get what?"

I let out a small, humourless chuckle. "You got your vengeance the second my mother died in childbirth. She was his true love, and he has to live every day knowing he could have prevented it or at least been there at the end. Instead, she died alone. You can kill me, but it won't have the effect you think it will. Lorenzo has been broken for a long time. You can't take any more away from him."

There, a nice dose of psychobabble to confuse the situation and, hopefully, the man tipping precariously to one side.

"My being here is a constant reminder of what he lost. When you kill me, he never has to look at my face again. A face that resembles my mother so closely. You'd be letting him off the hook."

I put some anger in my voice, because it occurs to me that I'm on to something good. If I can convince Giani that

I hate Lorenzo as much as him, he may deviate from his plan. I can see his cogs turning. His booze-soaked mind is trying to make sense of what I'm saying.

"How could you ever think of letting him get away with what he did?" I continue with venom coating every word. "He deprived me of a mother!" I shriek. "I never knew what her smile looked like, or if she would have sung me to sleep. I never got to learn how to be a woman from her. He took that from me. All the memories a child should have when they are grown, I never had and never will. So, think about it before you do something rash. Be smart, Mr Arello. Help me punish him until the day he dies."

Oh wow, this is an Oscar-worthy performance if I do say so myself. I might ask Pete if I can join his theatre group when we get back.

"You hate him?" Giani asks, a tinge of wonder in his voice.

"With everything I have," I reply quickly.

Reaching around, he plucks a gun I hadn't noticed from the waistband of his trousers. It's shocking the Mafiosi haven't blown their own butts off. I'm sure it's not safe gun protocol to wedge it down your ass crack.

Placing it on the table next to him, he pulls out a chair and sits. It's the first time since he began speaking that

I feel I can breathe a little easier. My eyes scan the room as he pours himself a glass of wine. We're in a dilapidated living room. The walls are stone and they look old—an old farmhouse, maybe.

Surprisingly, he slides the glass over to me before snapping his fingers at the man standing by the door. The other man dutifully retrieves another glass for his boss. I probably shouldn't drink given I definitely have a slight concussion. I take a large gulp anyway.

"I find myself surprised by you, Bonnie."

"Ditto," I say over my glass.

"Lorenzo is a coward. I would never have let Maria go. If you had been mine, you would have stayed with me no matter what," he says with conviction.

The thought of Giani ever being my dad sends a shiver down my spine. It's not his sleazebag character that makes me feel queasy. It's the cruelty I know he possesses. My life would have been hell if he'd got his hands on me.

"Would..." I purposefully let my question trail off. I want him interested in me.

"Speak, child," he urges, drinking his own wine.

"If you'd found my mother before I was born, would you have taken me on as your own?"

"Of course," he barks, slamming a meaty hand to the table. "Maria would have had to be punished, you understand, but I would never have hurt her child. I would have raised you as my own. Taught you everything you needed to succeed."

Oh, how chivalrous! Douchebag.

Okay, time to bring it home. "I would have had a proper family," I choke, my hand flying to my mouth. The single tear is a bonus. I'd like to say it's my wonderful acting skills again, but it's the pain radiating from my face that's making my eyes water. Whatever works, right? And it *has* worked. I know I have him now. Giani Arello won't lay a finger on me. I just have to work out how the hell I use his newfound soft-spot-slash-weakness to get myself out of here!

28

Allegra

A WELCOME STATE OF calm descends on me as I ready myself to leave. After all the turmoil I've felt recently, it's nice to feel in control again. I'm in my comfort zone.

I'm sure Giani expects me to go racing after him, and I will, just not how he thinks. Bonnie is safe for now. Her voice is also whispering in my ear. I was ready to go for the jugular—literally. The second I saw she was gone I wanted to physically hurt the Arellos. But now, I know that's not the way. I can't imagine what Bonnie would think of me if I did things the way I would have in my younger days. Giani is a bad guy who deserves everything he gets. But he's also a person, and no amount of reasoning would convince Bonnie I was right to kill him. I know that much about her.

Giani won't hurt her until he has an audience. This whole show is for Lorenzo. Giani wants to see him suffer.

He'll want to look Lorenzo in the eye when he kills Bonnie. So, we have time and I'll use it wisely. I'm going to dismantle his life within the hour.

While Giani has been plotting and planning to pull off his little stunt, I have taken the time to worm my way into all his affairs. I knew something was coming, and even though I couldn't go after him until he went and made the first move, that didn't mean I had to sit idly by.

"We're ready," Toni says when I reach the bottom step. Rosa, Mia, and Toni are all dressed in the same black combats and T-shirts. They're ready for what's to come.

"Rosa, I want you and Mia to go to Giani's warehouse. Burn it to the ground."

She nods and they leave. "Toni, we're going to go pay Gisto a visit."

The pact with the Arellos is null and void. Giani knew it would happen, but I doubt he's fully grasped the consequences of his actions yet. By night's end, he will have.

Toni jumps into the driver's seat. We're ten minutes away from Gisto's house. He won't be expecting us because he'll have no idea what his father planned or executed. Giani has never put his faith in his son and it's going to bite him in the ass.

We roll up to the monstrosity of a house with no opposition. Gisto has his own security, but they spend their nights drinking the contents of Gisto's cave rather than patrolling the grounds. It's just another example of the family's idiocy. They think they're untouchable. With the current pact, there is no one who would dare attack them. And to an extent, I agree. The Arellos are one of the Mafiosi families. There is no one on this island, or in Italy for that matter, who would do something as stupid as provoke them, let alone attack in the dead of the night.

But as I said, the pact is no longer in play. If Giani had any sense of love or loyalty to his son, he would've forewarned him.

We cut the engine and exit the car with practised efficiency. I've studied the layout of Gisto's place and know exactly where to find him. He'll be passed out in his office after drinking himself into a coma. His wife will be asleep after feigning a headache as a way of rejecting his drunken advances.

I pick the lock and tread lightly through the foyer. All is quiet, just as I thought it would be. With our guns drawn, we head straight for the office. A dimmed light casts shadows over the dark wood. It's an oppressive space. Gisto is snoring like a freight train on the couch. Thankfully, he isn't as portly as his father. Toni won't have a problem moving him.

I lean against the wall and watch Toni slap a piece of duct tape over his mouth. Gisto's bleary eyes flicker open, but his brain is slow to catch up. Toni has already dragged him off the couch to the floor before he realises what's happening. There is a string of muffled words pouring out of Gisto's mouth, but they mean nothing to me. He can rant and rave all he likes.

"Take him," I say, and lead the way out and back to the car. Toni dumps Gisto in the boot. He slides back into the driver's seat and waits for my next directive.

"To the docks."

We're halfway there when I receive a message from Rosa. It simply reads: "Done." Once again, the Arellos' cockiness will be their undoing. Giani has his pudgy fingers in many nasty pies. Unfortunately, he didn't think separating his cargo was a necessity. He stores all his products in the same place. That place is now in flames. He's just lost millions.

Our next stop is his dockyard site office. My spies found out he keeps all the titles and deeds to his business and land stored in the floor safe at the docks. He operates his underground businesses from a shell company. It's the first smart thing he's done. Now that I know about it, I'm going to rob him blind. No deeds and titles, means no power. I plan to take everything he has.

The dockyard will be a little harder to get into, but I have faith my mole inside will work his magic. I sent him a coded message as soon as we left with Gisto. If he does his job, Giani's men will be expecting us. They'll think we're there for a meeting. My man will escort us to the office and volunteer to guard us until Giani arrives.

Of course, one phone call to their boss would scupper the plan, but I'm betting on them being too scared to check in. Ruling with fear only goes so far. Eventually, the people you rely on are too afraid to question anything. That's what I'm banking on with Giani's dockyard security.

There's one guy standing at the barrier to the entrance. As most of the families have business here, we have designated areas. I've never visited the south side. Nico, Marco, and Franco have invited me to their respective offices a time or two, as I have them. That's the mark of our trust. It isn't a coincidence none of us have had an invitation to Giani's place and vice versa. He was always on the outside.

Toni slows to a stop and lowers the window a few inches. "Donna Malgeri. We should be expected."

I'm not the named Donna yet, but I love Toni for using my title. He's showing me his respect and I appreciate it now more than ever.

The guard waves us through, pointing to a building in the distance. "Benny will wait with you," he replies. Benny is my guy on the inside. He's done well.

Gisto is trying to call out, but his pleas fall on deaf ears. Toni parks around the side of the building, hiding the car in the shadows. We need to get Gisto into the office without being seen. Benny directs us to a side door, almost hidden behind a stack of crates. We can't take too long. If the guard notices we haven't entered through the main office door, he'll get suspicious.

Benny and Toni work quickly. They shove Gisto through the side door and we're out front within seconds. I see the guard looking over, but I pay him no mind—It would be strange if I did—before stepping through the main entrance.

Inside, Gisto is wriggling, doing his level best to break free. Toni drags him over to Giani's office chair with ease.

"Gisto. I'm going to have Toni remove the tape. If you make a sound, you die. Is that clear?" My voice is low and deadly. Gisto nods. "I won't give you a second warning, so bear that in mind." As I speak, I unholster my gun.

Nodding to Toni, I settle back against the door. The sound of the tape being ripped off almost makes my eyes water. I'm sure Gisto just lost half his facial hair.

"What is this, Allegra?" he asks quietly. I'm happy he's taken my warning seriously.

I decide to answer his question with one of my own. "Do you know what your father did this evening, Gisto?"

He looks between me and Toni. "No. But I presume from this, it isn't good."

Well, give the man a prize. "Tonight, your father broke the pact."

Gisto shakes his head disbelievingly. "He wouldn't—"

"But he did," I interject. "Didn't you wonder why he had you mess with our cargo with the intention of getting caught?"

Gisto swallows hard. Beads of sweat form on his brow. "All he said was we needed to send a message to Lorenzo."

"Indeed," I say. "I'm guessing he left out the real reason. Do you know Bonnie Moorside?"

He shakes his head. "Never heard of her."

"Do you know the reason your father hates Lorenzo so much?"

"Old family shit, I think."

I sigh. "Gisto, my dear man. You really are in the dark, aren't you?"

He bristles but doesn't reply. I proceed to fill him in on Giani and Lorenzo's history. By the time I'm finished, Gisto's head has dropped to his chest.

"You're telling me he's broken the pact for a whore he loved decades ago?" he growls.

"Careful, Gisto. Maria is Bonnie's mother and Bonnie means a lot to me. I don't think you want to use that particular word to describe her, especially not when I know what your wife gets up to."

His face pales and then turns a shade of red I'm not sure is medically possible.

"Do you want to cut to the chase and let me tell you why I have you here?"

"You plan to kill me, right? Exact your own revenge," he says matter-of-factly.

I laugh loudly. "Gisto, your father wouldn't give a shit if I killed you. We both know that."

It's sad to watch his reaction. No child should know their parent sees them as nothing more than a burden.

"Then why?"

"Because as much as I dislike you, I think I can help you out."

He scoffs. "Why bother? I know you well enough, Allegra. You'll burn us to the ground for his actions."

I tip my head and smile. "You do know me well. However, I'm going to need your help to do it, and in return, I'll let you walk away with some dignity. Your father will have to answer to the Mafiosi for his actions. I can make it so you, your wife, and your children are left out of it."

"And my brother?" Ah, here he is, Giani's son. He's got a nasty streak just like his father. "What about him? What if I don't want him saved?"

"Then he won't be. I know you've never been trusted with your father's secrets. But I also know you're a slippery son of a bitch, and I'll bet my Ferrari you've made it your business to know certain things—like the combination to his floor safe."

He gets a glint in his eyes. "I'll make a deal," he begins. "I'll give you the combination if you leave me with the house I'm in and enough money to live on."

I rub my chin. "What will you do for business? There will be no work here, and I plan to blacklist your family name. That's not up for negotiation."

He shrugs. "Allegra, believe it or not, I couldn't give a flying fuck about this goddamn life. All it's ever brought is pain. I want enough money for my kids to grow up in a secure home. I'll find legitimate work if I have to."

I contemplate his request for a few seconds. More than anything, I'm surprised to hear how unhappy he is. Of course, Giani made his life hell, but I never thought he disliked "The Life" itself.

"Deal. Now—the safe code."

Gisto calls it out as I tap it into the keypad. The satisfying click makes me smile. I have Giani's entire life in my hands. Flicking through, I find the deed to Gisto's house and hand it over.

"Once I have control of the Arello accounts, I'll have your money transferred. Fair?"

"Fair. I hope this is the last time we have to do business, Allegra."

"Same. Now let's put on a show. I need the man at the gate to think I'm pissed off at being stood up. Sadly, Gisto, you need to go back the way you came and into the trunk."

"As long as you get me home, I'll do whatever you want."

I couldn't have foreseen how successful my plan would be. I'm a little shocked, to be honest. Then again, I am Allegra Malgeri. I strive for perfection.

Handing the paperwork to Toni, I instruct him to get it to my money man. Reggio will have all of Giani's assets transferred to me within a day. And then it's game over for the Arello family.

In the meantime, it's time to visit the man of the hour. I hope he's ready for me.

29

Bonnie

Wow, GIANI REALLY LIKES to talk once he gets going. And he really knows how to hold a grudge. No complaints here, though. While he's bitching about Lorenzo, he isn't thinking about hurting me. I throw in an "absolutely" and an "I hate him so much" now and then, which has kept him happy so far.

The guy who was standing guard at the door, and is built like a semi-detached house, has sat down and is thumbing through something on his phone. Giani has opened another bottle of wine and I'm sitting here praying I can keep him distracted long enough for Allegra to find me.

I've listened to him bitch about Lorenzo, Allegra, my mother, his sons, and his wife. How the hell anyone can stand to be around him is astonishing. He's delighted in retelling stories of times he punished his kids and wife. He's a narcissist and also a sociopath. It reminds me of how dangerous life here is.

Being cooped up in the villa made me forget—or at least blinded me to—the reality of Allegra and Lorenzo's life in Sicily. All because I haven't witnessed the seedy underbelly, doesn't mean it isn't there. I know Allegra went to the docks several times. What happened there? Did she have to *deal* with someone? Is there a version of Allegra where she becomes someone closer to Giani? I can't imagine it. Yet again, I could never imagine meeting real mobsters.

"I can't wait to see the look in his eyes," Giani slurs. He's said the same thing several times already. I don't even need to answer. He's lost in his own miserable world.

The more he drinks, the more confident I become thinking I could escape. Giani untied my hands a while ago so I could have a drink with him. Mr Meaty is so engrossed in his phone, I think I could reach the unlocked door before he registered what was happening. Giani is pissed as a fart, so no worries there. It's just the man outside. I'm guessing *he's not* drunk and is probably armed.

I'm halfway through a semi-decent plan to run when there's an almighty thud outside. The door shakes and then there's a scraping sound. Giani hasn't noticed, but Mr

Meaty did. He slips his phone back into his pocket and retrieves his gun. He can't be that worried, though, because he hasn't risen from his seat.

It all happens so fast. The door bursts open and there's two muted pops. Mr Meaty falls to the floor screaming, clutching both knees. My head whips back to the door where Toni is standing, gun raised. Moving with a grace and speed I didn't think a bloke of that stature could, he swoops in, slaps some tape on Mr Meaty's face, and begins dragging him out of the room.

Giani staggers off his chair, but he's in no fit state to do anything. I use the opportunity to slip out of reach. I've now got a couch and table between us. He won't get to me before Toni gets back, and it doesn't look like he knows what to do, really. His head snaps from me, to the door, and back. Panic and confusion are outweighing the intoxication of too much wine.

Like an avenging angel, Allegra steps through the door dressed all in black. Her hair is scraped back into that ferocious bun I've come to like. Weird how a hairstyle can convey so much power.

Giani finally comes to his senses and picks up the gun from the table. Our little bonding session is, by all accounts, over as he aims the pistol at me. His hands are unsteady and

I'm not convinced he'd hit me if he pulled the trigger, but I really don't want to find out.

"Where is he?" Giani spits.

Allegra grimaces. "Lorenzo is at home, where I told him to be. *Tut tut*, Giani, you have made a mess."

She's so calm, it's unnerving. I expected her to burst in here with the heat of a thousand suns, but this is worse. She's oozing power, and her eyes are dark with malice. I swallow. Even when Allegra came for me and got angry, she wasn't like this. I think I'm finally seeing Donna Malgeri, and I'm not sure if I like it.

"How did you find us? I didn't send the message yet," Giani growls and then hiccups.

"Giani, you're as predictable as you are round. It's astonishing you've been the head of your family for so long. Of course you'd take Bonnie to the house you were supposed to live in with Maria. It's all so dramatic."

"She was mine!" he roars.

"And Bonnie is mine," Allegra seethes. "There's no coming back from this, Arello."

Allegra still hasn't looked at me. Her statement of me being hers hits me in the chest with force. I've never had anyone declare I belonged to them like that. The feminist in me is crossing her arms and scowling, but the other part of me...the part that wants to be loved wholeheartedly by someone, mewls in pleasure—not that Allegra loves me or anything.

Toni re-enters the room, his gun trained on Giani. This is going to turn into a bloodbath if everyone starts shooting. Stepping from behind the couch, I draw everyone's attention to me. I watch Allegra scan my face and her eyes darken with anger as she pauses over the bruise I know is developing on my cheek.

"He laid hands on you?" she asks in a voice so low I barely hear her.

"No, I fell out of the van. Giani didn't hit me."

"You and me, dyke," Giani suddenly barks. "We finish it. If Lorenzo's too much of a coward to face me, I'll be happy to put you in the ground instead of him."

For crying out loud.

Allegra sneers and steps forward. "Agreed."

"No!" I scream. "No, that's enough!" Allegra flicks her gaze to me momentarily. "Allegra, you found me. I just want to go home. Please."

Her jaw flexes and her nose flares. She's not happy, but I don't care. I can't watch her do something we'd never recover from.

"Nico, Franco, and Marco are on their way. Giani's future lies in their hands now," she eventually says.

I don't know what that means, but from the way Giani grips the edge of the seat he's been using to keep himself upright, I don't think these men coming here is a good thing for him.

Puffing out his chest in one last attempt to seem in control, Giani slashes his hand in the air, and declares, "This has nothing to do with them."

"You broke the pact, Giani. No family members, remember? Your grudge is over three decades old *and* you took an innocent. I ignored the attempts on our business dealings, but this? No. It's time to face judgement."

"So, you're a coward too, huh? Just like a Ferrante. He taught you well. It's a shame. Your parents would turn in their grave at your lack of backbone."

He's goading her, and for a split second, I think he's said enough to force her to react with violence. Allegra's hand twitches on her gun, but she takes a deep breath and looks at me.

"If it's any consolation, I hope they spare your life, Arello."

"Why? I'll come for you. This isn't over until I have Lorenzo begging for mercy and you on your back like the filthy whore you are. I'll show you what a real man can do."

I roll my eyes. Allegra looks at Toni and then at me, before bursting out in laughter. "You couldn't show a blow-up doll a good time, Giani, but that's beside the point. I'll answer your question. I want them to spare you, so you live to see everything you own taken from you. With the help of Gisto, who it seems has grown tired of your bullshit, I now own everything: your businesses, houses, yacht...all of it is mine."

He balls his fists. "You're lying."

"No, I'm not. If you'd have spent even half the time tending to business and family the way you did this trite abduction, you'd still have a life to live here. But you didn't, and now it's all gone."

I can see his massive hulk vibrating with anger. The cold fury Allegra possessed when she first walked in has now transformed into an evil grin. Just her facial expression is enough to twist the knife in Giani's gut.

The air changes in an instant and I know what's about to happen. My dads would say I'm stupid for putting myself in harm's way, but when I see Giani shift almost imperceptibly, my instincts take over and I dive toward Allegra. Our bodies slam together as the deafening thunder of Giani's gun going off, booms through the room.

We're on the floor, and my ears are ringing. I feel hands grab my shoulders and lift me off her. For a moment, I'm scared it's Giani, but the overwhelming odour of Toni's cologne settles my nerves.

Stumbling back, I take in the scene. Giani is on his knees, clutching his shoulder. Red liquid seeps through his fingers. Toni is hauling Allegra up, patting down every inch of her body, looking for a gunshot wound. She swats his hands away and pushes past him until she's in front of me. Her hands roam frantically over my body. "Are you hurt?" she asks urgently.

I feel sore but nothing hurts badly. "I'm fine."

Cars skid to a halt outside and multiple doors open and close. Allegra pulls me into her body and holds me. Noise erupts all around us as men pile in. They're all dressed in fine Italian suits.

"Get him up," the older of the men barks. Toni reaches for Giani and pulls him up to his feet.

"Let's go," Allegra whispers in my ear. "You don't want to see this."

No, I don't. Giani is an animal, but does that mean he deserves to die?

"Allegra, what would you like us to do?" another man asks.

She shakes her head as she moves us towards the door. "That's not my decision. You know I cannot pass judgement fairly. I'll accept whatever punishment you see fit, Nico. Goodnight."

Tucked into Allegra's body, I let her lead me to her car. Toni follows moments later. We slip inside without a word. Up to this point, Allegra has looked in complete control. That is, until she meets my eyes in the back of the car and she breaks. She sobs as her hands reach for my face.

Toni drives without a backward glance. The only thing I can do is fold myself into her body. She hauls me onto her lap and buries her face in my neck.

"I'm okay," I repeat into her ear, but it's like she can't accept it. Her fingers grip me harder, as though she expects me to vanish.

"I'm sorry—so sorry, Bonnie," she cries.

Stroking her hair, I kiss the top of her head. Toni pulls the car around the back of the villa. "We're home," he says.

I look out the window and see my parents running towards the car. Allegra sucks in a breath and breaks away from me. She wipes her eyes and I see the mask slip back on.

"Go to them," she says, but I don't want to move. "Go, Bonnie." Her voice is strong and commanding once again.

The car door is ripped open, and I have little choice but to get out. My dads envelop me in their arms. Kelley and Pete aren't far behind. I'm passed between the group as they cry and hold me tightly. I try to look back at Allegra, but she's gone. A flash of platinum hair entering the house is all I have left of her.

"Come on, pumpkin. Let's get you inside."

I'm chauffeured into the kitchen. Lorenzo stands waiting, his eyes wide with alarm, and I know he wants to hug me. I reach out my arm and pull him in. I feel a connection to him I wasn't aware had been missing.

I know everyone in the room loves me and wants to make sure I'm okay, but the only thing I want to do is leave all of them and find Allegra. A sense of urgency rises in me. The threat of the Arello family is gone, and therefore, my need to be in Sicily is now gone, too. I can go home. I can go back to my life—a life without Allegra.

30

Allegra

MY HANDS ARE SHAKING violently as I crash through the door to my bedroom. The bravado I had used to get Bonnie back has evaporated. I feel raw. Donna Malgeri is gone. If ever I needed a wake-up call to finally push me into doing the right thing for myself, it was Bonnie being taken from me.

I was in control, as usual, until I spotted her in that room, her face bruised and her hair dishevelled. I was confident Giani wouldn't hurt her until he had an audience, but I could have been so wrong and she would have suffered if that had been the case. And it's all for nothing. None of this is worth Bonnie getting hurt. Egos and power plays are not important enough to pay the steep price. I thought being a Ferrante was worth the pain and sacrifice, but now I know it's not. I've proved myself to everyone, time and time again. I can stop now.

I love Lorenzo with all my heart. And I know he won't stop loving me for asking this of him. I need out. I'd hoped to reach a point where the Ferrante family name was known for its good business practices instead of our role in the Mafiosi. There is still work to do before that dream can be a reality. I don't think I can wait that long.

I'm not sure if Bonnie wants more than these last few weeks with me, but I intend to find out. First, I need to speak with Lorenzo before I chicken out. His office is in darkness when I arrive and begin pacing. It won't be long until he arrives, though. Lorenzo might not be the head of the house, but old habits die hard. Poring over meaningless paperwork keeps his mind occupied as he adjusts to his new normal. I think I'm about to blow up his new normal into something neither of us recognise.

As predicted, Lorenzo walks in half an hour later. The constant back and forth has helped expel some of my nervous energy. He looks pale and, somehow, older. I pour us both a drink as he sinks into his office chair.

"Drink," I say, pushing the tumbler into his hand.

We both throw back the amber liquid and sigh. "Thank you, Allegra. I owe you everything."

"I'm not sure you'll be thanking me after tonight."

He leans back and surveys me as I sit opposite him. "Did something happen with Giani?"

I shake my head. "No... Yes. Too much has happened, Lorenzo."

"What do you mean? Tell me, Allegra."

I brace myself. "I want out, Lorenzo." He stares at me. "I don't want to be officially named as the Donna to the Ferrante family."

"Where is this coming from? It's *all* you've ever wanted. You told me that many times."

I can't fault him for being confused. He's right. It's what I strived for every day of my life with him—until recently.

Where do I begin to get him to understand? "You know I've been pulling us away from the more traditional work this family is used to."

He's not a stupid man, and I'm not naïve enough to think he never peeked at the books or the everyday running of the family businesses. He nods.

I continue, "I told myself it was the smart play. We both know, as we've discussed before, the feds are a hair's breadth away from taking us down. It's inevitable. The only way to save our family from prison is to cut ties—be fully legit in everything we do and hope they can't pin any of our past transgressions on us."

"And you've achieved that?"

"Apart from the art shipments."

He shrugs. "Out of everything that goes on around here, a bit of art theft is nothing."

"Sure, until you realise we're still dealing with the same hazards. We still have to operate with dangerous people. *We* have to be dangerous people. And I don't want to be that, Lorenzo—not anymore. I don't want to have to be the Ice Bitch for the rest of my life. It took meeting Bonnie to really understand that."

"Bonnie? What's she got to do with it? Her life is in the UK."

I nod. "It started with her abduction and how much of a colossal fuck up it all was. I hated how she looked at me and I hated how I acted. I was angry and made mistakes. But the worst part of it was the anger itself. I'd started losing myself, only seeing value in the power I could attain. Whether or not we managed to get away from the Mafiosi label didn't matter. I focused all my energy on proving my worthiness of acquiring and holding the Donna title."

"But you've never had a problem with our lifestyle."

"I didn't know any better, Lorenzo. I didn't know I wanted anything different."

"Until Bonnie showed up."

"Yes. We grew close. Once she stopped fighting me, we talked—got to know each other a little."

"And more?" he asks.

"Yes. But she doesn't belong in this world. I wouldn't want her to. You must feel the same."

He closes his eyes briefly. "No, I don't want her in it either, and I promised her fathers she'd never get caught up in it again."

"So tell me this, Lorenzo: How do you expect to have a relationship with her while you're still here, living the life of a mob boss?"

"I don't. It's a decision I've been wrestling with."

Ah, so I'm not the only member of this family needing a change.

"And what did you decide?"

Rubbing his forehead, he chuckles, "I thought I could have the best of both worlds. I could leave the family here in your capable hands and take time away to get to know my daughter."

"No, Lorenzo. It doesn't work like that. If your name is still associated with the mob, she will always be in danger.

The pact only holds so much weight. There are families across the globe that could come calling for a power grab or revenge. The list is endless. We've done well up to now, keeping ourselves on the right side of things. Forgetting Giani, we don't have any foes. But the longer we stay in this business, the greater the chance of us developing one. That's not even taking in the fact the police could use her for their own gains. She'd never be free."

"Keeping the family legacy alive is all I've ever known, Allegra."

"Your family legacy will mean nothing if we let her down again. Bonnie is the only legacy you should be concerned with."

"And the rest of the family?"

"I'll deal with them," I say. It might take a bit of time, but I will get them to see reason. "Most of them are off travelling around the world, living a life of luxury. They have no idea how to run this family and deal with the consequences of it. It's time to educate them. I'm sure there will be no arguments after that."

"You really want this? What will you do? What will any of us do?"

I smile. "Lorenzo, nothing will change in the day to day. Everyone has a job to do. They'll just have less shitty ones."

He gets up and pours us both another drink. "It's going to take time. There will be a lot of pissed off and confused people to deal with on the outside. If we're going to do this, we do it right. A clean break from it all, with no backlash."

"Absolutely. There's no point otherwise."

"I didn't think we'd end up here," he says.

I nod in agreement. "Neither did I, but then again, I wasn't expecting Bonnie."

"She really got to you, huh?"

I can feel myself getting hot. "She has, and I don't want to mess it up. She's the only woman I've seen myself having a real future with."

It's true, and it scares me to death.

Lorenzo's eyes well with tears. "Those Poletti women will get you every time. Maria had me under her spell from the first time I saw her. Bonnie did the same to you, I think."

I laugh. "Well, she did...after all the arguing and bitching."

"No, that was all part of the attraction, I'm sure. If it means anything to you, Allegra, I'm happy for you both."

I finish my second drink. "She hasn't said she wants more with me yet."

"She will. You're Allegra Malgeri," he says with a wink. "Don't waste time wondering. Talk to her now. Get it all out there. I would give anything for a few more seconds with Maria. Don't let another minute pass by without pouring out your heart to her if she's the one, *bella*."

In an unusual display of affection, Lorenzo pulls me into a hug. He's warm and feels like home.

"Thank you, *papà*," I whisper. He kisses my head.

I leave him to his own thoughts. Mine are entirely on Bonnie. I need to see her again and reassure myself she is okay. The kitchen is empty. Maybe I should wait until the morning, because I'm sure her dads are making a fuss over her right now. What if she doesn't want to see me? It wouldn't be a complete surprise if she blamed me for all this craziness.

I'm totally lost in thought when I round the corner and run straight into her. We both fall backwards and hit the ground with a thud.

"Crap," she mumbles.

I scramble to get to her. "Are you okay? Did I hurt you?"

Her hair is a mess, and her eyes are red-rimmed from crying. I'm sure it's been an emotional few hours. A knot tightens in my stomach. I'm the reason she's gone through so much. I'm being selfish wanting more from her.

"Stop," she says. Her fingers brush my cheek. "I was on my way to find you. Can we talk?"

Pulling her up, I resist the urge to take her in my arms. We walk to my room, but I pause. "We can go somewhere else if you want."

"Here's fine. I'm not scared, Allegra."

She's the strongest woman I've ever met.

"Okay," I respond with hope blooming in my chest.

The cleaning crew have been in and removed any evidence of a scuffle. At least Bonnie won't have to see her friends' blood on the floor.

"How is your head?" I ask. She's got a black eye, which makes me want to reevaluate my stance on letting the other families decide Giani's fate. I should hav—

"Allegra, stop. I can see your jaw clenching. You'll have no back teeth if you keep it up."

"You're hurt and it's my fault."

"No, it's Giani's fault. I don't want you holding that kind of anger in. Please." She stands in front of me and places both palms on my chest. "It's over."

Resting my head against hers, I breathe in deeply. Her scent calms me. "Do you want to talk about it?"

"Not tonight. I've already gone over it so many times, I'm exhausted."

"Then let's sleep."

I want to talk to her—ask her if she sees a future with me, but we're both bone-tired. If I get to sleep next to her one more time, I'll be happy.

We slip under the sheets without a stitch of clothing on and fold into each other. When I wake, I'm alone. The sun is shining and the house is alive with people going about their business. Stretching, my ears hone in on Kelley's voice outside my room.

"Bonnie, the plane leaves in two hours. Will you get moving? Pete's getting really annoying. I need you to be my buffer."

The plane's leaving in two hours? What plane?

Rolling out of bed, I search for something suitable to wear. I haven't got time to get dressed up as usual, but I won't parade around in a silk robe for all and sunder to see. Snagging on a pair of silk sleep trousers and a tank top, I step outside into the corridor. Bonnie's door is open a fraction. Knocking, I push it open and take in the sight before me.

Large suitcases are open on the bed and they're stuffed with the clothes I had put in her wardrobes. Bonnie is sitting at the vanity with her arms folded and a scowl on her face. Phillip and Mark busy themselves with her belongings.

"Bonnie?"

"Allegra."

"We have to go," Phillip says, his voice icy. "It's time for Bonnie to come home, where she's safe."

Ignoring him, I walk over to her. "You're leaving?"

She shoots a scornful look over my shoulder and pulls me back to my room.

"They're not listening to reason," she begins. "Yesterday terrified them, and now it's all blowing up. Pop and Dad marched into my room this morning and just started packing. I heard them and went to see what all the fuss was about. I'm sorry I didn't wake you."

My mind is foggy with sleep and the aftereffects of yesterday's stress. "I... Do you want to go?"

She squeezes my hands. "I *do* need to go home. But I wasn't expecting it to be like this."

I want to tell her to stay for a little while longer. I'm not ready to say goodbye. Everything is happening too fast.

"Can I call you?" How pathetic.

"Of course you can. I'd be upset if you didn't. And maybe when they've calmed down a bit, I can come back and visit. Or you can come to me."

Her tone and words aren't aligning with how I thought she felt. This seems so final; like two friends saying goodbye, promising to keep in touch but never following through.

Is this really it? The end of our story?

31

Bonnie

MY HEART HURTS. LEAVING the villa is the last thing I wanted to do, but how could I say no to my dads? They were so afraid for me; they broke down several times. I'd never seen them like that.

But then I picture Allegra's face that morning, and how her eyes became frantic at the sight of my parents packing for me. I had a choice. And now I think I made the wrong one. Instead of telling her how I felt, I thought it was better to leave it unsaid, parting as friends, instead of heartbroken lovers who'd only just started getting to know each other.

The logical side of my brain told me at the time, it was for the best. I needed to see if my feelings for her were true and not just the response to a trauma. I could kick my own arse for it, though. Instead of following my heart, I let my head and my dads' influences take over.

It's been three weeks since I left and I haven't heard from Allegra even once. We traded one consolatory kiss at the villa door and then I left. I couldn't bring myself to text her at the airport or when we arrived home. It was all too much.

My parents have finally gone back to their lives after a heated discussion this morning. They've been full-on for weeks, and I got to the end of my tether when *they* were deciding if I should go back to work or not.

Suffice to say, they were not pleased when I kicked them out of my flat. But it had to be done—for my sanity and for our relationship.

"Morning, sunshine," Kelley chirps. She's been managing the bookshop since we returned from Italy. Clive was suspiciously okay with me being away for so long without giving him notice. The brand-new car and watch he's flashing around gives me a clue as to his behaviour. I'm sure the Ferrantes lined his pockets to keep him quiet and compliant. I won't complain. It's given me plenty of time to work through what happened.

A part of me is desperate to know what's going on over there. I want to know what happened to Giani. Is he still a threat? Is he still alive? What does it all mean for Allegra?

No matter how hard I try, I can't get her out of my head. I've stopped admitting that out loud as to avoid Pete bursting out into song. I love Kylie Minogue, but I can't hear one more rendition of *Can't Get You Out of My Head*.

"Morning, Kel."

"Happy to be back?" She dumps her bag in the back and walks out with two coffees in a tray. "I brought you a welcome-back latte."

"Ah, you didn't have to, but I appreciate it. I've had a rough morning."

"Pops and Dad?"

"Bingo!"

"Wanna talk about it?"

I shake my head. "Nope. I want to talk about anything but that, thanks."

"Okay. The new Bagman book is out tomorrow. Wanna talk about that?"

The bell jingles above the shop door and Janice prances in. "Oh, you're back!"

"I am." This is the last interaction I want to have right now, but Clive still won't fire her, so I have no choice.

"Are you the boss again?"

"I'm back in my role as store manager."

"Huh. Great. Well, *boss*, I need to take the afternoon off. I have a dentist appointment."

"You've had seven this year, Janice. I can't authorise any more paid time off. I'll get your shift covered but it will be unpaid leave."

I've had enough of her shit to last a lifetime. If the one thing I take away from my time with Allegra and the Mob, it's standing up for myself more.

"Clive—"

"Isn't in charge. Now, I have work to do and so do you. Start by unloading the new releases in the kids' section. When you've done that, you can man the till."

Janice stalks off with a murderous stare at me. I look at her with boredom until she's out of eyesight.

Audrey suddenly rounds the corner, beaming. "That was fantastic. Way to stand up to the silly old cow, Bonnie."

"When did you get here?" We're not even officially open yet.

"Oh, I nipped in behind Kelley. I wanted to get my hands on the second Loch & Key book. Love me some vampires. The sex is hot, too."

"It's a sapphic collection," Kelley replies with raised eyebrows.

"And it's hot. Mmm, give me a bit of Amelia Loch, any day of the week."

"I'm just gonna..." I point my thumb over my shoulder at nothing in particular. I don't want to listen to whatever Audrey is about to say next. She's got zero boundaries sometimes.

It's nice to be back in the shop, surrounded by books. It's the only time I've felt a sense of peace in the past three weeks. My heart thuds particularly hard when I think about the other place that made me feel at peace: in Allegra's arms.

Silly, really. I've been away from her longer than I knew her. Surely, I should be over it; maybe even glad I dodged a bullet—literally. The old me would have been. That version of me would have rejoiced at getting back to her routine and the safety of the known. Somewhere along the way, though, that version of me vanished and now I don't know what to do with myself.

I still love reading, but I'm not consumed by it. My thoughts wander to Italy more often than not. The microwave meals don't hit the spot anymore, either. How could they possibly compare after eating the fine Italian cuisine? Everything is a little duller since coming home.

"Look what I found under the till," Kelley says, breaking my daydreams. She hands me my copy of *Mob's Seduction*. "We never did finish it."

"I did. Allegra read it with me."

It's the first time I've spoken her name out loud. Kelley nibbles her lip in discomfort. She's trying to figure out what to say next.

"I'll pass over the fact you finished a joint read with someone else. Are you ready to talk about her?"

"What's to talk about?"

"So, not ready, then."

"No, I'm serious. We could've had something if our lives were compatible. But they weren't—they aren't—and now I have to move on."

The door jingles again. Kelley eyes me but doesn't comment. She simply heads back to the till and to the customer who just walked in.

"Um, Bonnie, can you come here, please?" The quiver in her voice has me on high alert. My first thought is Giani. What if he's here? "Now, Bonnie," she calls.

I rush to the front of the shop, ready to fight, when my legs almost give out. Standing by the door, looking as striking as ever, is Allegra. She gives me a shy smile, and it takes everything in me not to run into her arms. Her eyes wander down to the book I'm still gripping; the book that helped us bond.

"The book with the terrible title," she says with a smile.

"A-Allegra, hi."

"Hello, Bonnie. How are you?"

"Um, fine thanks. You?"

Jesus, this is painful and unnecessary. The woman's been inside me, for crying out loud. There's no reason we should talk like strangers. And yet, I can't find it in me to say anything else in case it breaks the spell and she leaves.

"Have you got time to talk? I can come back later."

"She can talk now," Kelley interrupts. "It's good to see you, Al."

Al? Since when did they become bosom buddies?

"Kelley, I'm at work," I say for an unknown reason, because I do, in fact, want to talk to her. It's the only thing I want to do. Sadly, it's my knee-jerk reaction to do the opposite of what someone tells me to do. I'm a work in progress.

"I'll come back," Allegra says, and I don't miss the hint of disappointment.

"No, wait. I can talk. Come with me." Turning, I head for the office. Butterflies and all manner of other winged creatures take flight in my stomach as I lead her to the cramped, windowless room.

My palms are sweaty, and I pray I'm not getting upper lip sweat too.

Not very attractive, Bonnie.

"You're wearing the clothes," she says quietly.

I fidget for a second. "They're really nice clothes."

I cast out all my wool the second I got home.

"You look beautiful."

My face heats. "What did you want to talk about?"

"May I?" she asks, pointing to the only other rickety chair in the room.

I nod, and she sits. My office chair squeaks embarrassingly as I lower myself into it. Allegra straightens her silk blouse and tucks her hair behind her ears. It's nice to see her looking more relaxed. I half expected to see the severe bun again.

"I'm sorry I haven't kept in touch. I've been rushed off my feet."

So, she's still running the family. I don't know why I expected anything else. It's her life.

"That's okay. The phone works both ways."

"I wanted to tell you why I've been busy," she says. I'm not sure I'm ready to hear about the family business again.

"Lorenzo and I have been working to break the Ferrante family away from the Mafiosi—cleanly."

"O-okay. I don't know what you mean by that."

She shuffles forward on her seat. "It means our business is no longer connected to the Mob. We're free. No more pacts, no more crime."

"Why? I mean, that's everything you and Lorenzo have wanted. You were on top, right?"

"And you know I was unhappy. Everything changed when I met you, Bonnie."

I can't believe my ears.

"I know you said you'd never marry a mob queen or become a sex slave to one," she says with a smile, "but would you be open to dating an Italian woman who loves fine wine and fashionable clothes? A woman who hasn't stopped thinking about you since the day she laid eyes on you in this very store?'

"You want to date me?" I'm aware my voice is higher than normal, and there is nothing I can do to control it, because I am flabbergasted and excited and ready to shout my joy from the rooftops.

"I want to date the hell out of you."

"What about the vineyard?"

"It's still going—stronger than ever, but I needed a break. I needed to come here and fight for my chance with you, Bonnie."

"You want to stay here? In the UK?"

"I'll stay wherever you want me to. Just say you'll give us a chance."

I'm on my feet in a nanosecond. Hell, yeah, I'm giving us a chance. She catches me as I launch myself into her lap. Taking her face in my hands, I kiss her hard. It's bruising and not exactly romantic, but I'm just happy she's here and wants me. There is plenty to talk about and I have a million questions, but they can wait.

"Is that a yes?" she mumbles in my mouth.

"A definite yes."

We're interrupted by Janice walking in. Her face is a picture of glee. "Wait until Clive—"

"Oh, *fuck off*, Janice."

She gapes at me. "Well, I never."

Standing up, I pull Allegra to her feet and out of the office. "Kelley, I'm taking the rest of the day off. You're in charge."

Is leaving professional? Nope. Do I care? Again—nope.

"Bon, we can wait until later," Allegra says, which makes me cackle like a Disney villain.

"Save your breath, Al. You're coming home with me. I've got three weeks of wasted sexy time to catch up on."

Allegra doesn't protest again. Kelley whoops and laughs. We walk down the street holding hands. I say "walk", but it's more like a quick march. By the time we reach my apartment, I'm out of breath, but a little wheezing won't stop me.

The door shuts behind us, and Allegra is on me; her body pinning me to the wall. "I've missed you."

Her tongue invades my mouth. She tastes how I remember, which ignites me even more. "Allegra, don't make me wait."

"Patience, princess," she coos.

"I'm not..." My words die on my tongue as she slips her hand up my skirt and shoves my knickers to one side.

"I might be out of the Mob, but I'm still the boss. Do you understand?"

Pretty sure I just came, to be honest.

"Yes, Donna Malgeri," I whimper. She growls and enters me. The force and speed have me singing to the ceiling in seconds.

I think back to the conversation I had with Kelley about Riley, the main character from *Mob's Seduction* falling in love with Mob Queen Leah, the day I met Allegra. I remember thinking how implausible it sounded. But then I got tossed into my own mafia romance, and here I am absolutely and irrevocably being seduced by a mobster.

I should write a book about it.

Epilogue

"Babe, you need to stop glaring at people like that!"

"I'm not glaring, Bonnie. I'm keeping an eye on them."

"You look like you're one misplaced book away from committing a homicide."

Allegra throws her hands in the air. "Would it really be that much of an imposition for people to put the book back where it belongs? It's just common decency. Those displays take a long time to create."

If Allegra catches me laughing, she'll stomp off in a huff, which will only make me laugh harder because she's adorable. I didn't realise how seriously she would take building displays. The new Selma Peterson book landed in the shop last week and Allegra asked if she could build the promotional book tower for it, which I had no problem with.

She did a fantastic job, but now she's guarding it like a case of rare wine. Only Audrey has had the bollocks to go over and peruse the display since opening this morning. Every other customer has seen Allegra standing ten feet away with hands on hips, glaring, and bustled off in another direction.

"It's the way things are, sweetie. But we need to sell the books, so you have to stop."

"Fine," she grumbles, "I'll go and make some tea."

When she's out of sight, I let my laughter go. God, I love that woman. It's been eighteen months of dates, holidays, and family meals. My dads took the longest time to come around to our relationship. Allegra never complained, though. She understood why they were finding it hard. Even after Allegra explained the Ferrante family was no longer in the Mafia, my fathers were sceptical.

I was at first, to be honest. I couldn't believe they were free and clear with no backlash. Thankfully, Allegra was patient and took me through every step she and Lorenzo took to reach the goal. They spent three gruelling weeks in meetings with the other Mafiosi families. They signed away client lists and territory rights.

The hardest part was convincing the Mafiosi they wouldn't turn informant. The only way to appease them was another pact. Allegra and Lorenzo swore they'd never turn state's evidence in return for a swift and complete breakaway from "The Life".

Apparently, the extended family gave no opposition as soon as they found out they'd get to keep their lavish lifestyles. It was Lorenzo's news that took me by surprise the most. He decided to drop the Ferrante name altogether, and with my blessing, adopted my mother's surname of Poletti. It was a way for him to prove to me he wanted a new beginning for us both. I knew what it meant for him to replace his family name with hers. I let him know what it meant to me, too.

Lorenzo visited a week after Allegra turned up, and like her, he never left. I kept waiting for the dream to end. I mean, who would give up a vineyard in Sicily to live in a cramped flat with a woman who works in a bookshop? Allegra, that's who. She wined and dined me and made me feel like *the only girl in the world*. Yes, I just sang that. Rihanna is the queen.

Anyway, we dated for a month before we became official girlfriends. Then, Allegra whisked me away for a holiday in Europe. We ended it with a week at the villa. Kelley met us there because, unbeknownst to me, she had never stopped hooking up with Beth. They're engaged now, and Kelley lives in Italy. It makes our book club a tad harder, but WhatsApp works well enough. Plus, Allegra is such a book nerd now. She squealed when Selma's new mob book released.

We binge-read it over homemade pizza and a bottle of Allegra's wine. It was perfect.

Now, though, I'm ready to make a change for us both. As much as Allegra is happy here, I know she misses the villa and working in the vineyard. I miss it too. Over the past few months, I've dipped my hand into the editing and proofreading pool. I figured I read enough, and for once I didn't want to stick to the known. I wanted to take a leaf out of Allegra's book and do something new; something scary. So I handed in my notice to Clive. I've got a few authors who want to work with me, so far. I can work from anywhere, so now I just have to tell Allegra we're going to Italy—if she wants to, which I think she does. Oh, blimey, I'm rambling internally.

Allegra slides up next to me with a cup. "Here, I made you tea. And look, I got it the right colour!"

"See? You're an expert. I knew you could do it, honey," I laugh.

"We're out of biscuits, though. I think Audrey is behind their disappearance."

"She works one afternoon a week, babe."

"And she's always got crumbs on her top when she comes back from her tea break."

"Speaking of working," I say, noticing Allegra's quirked eyebrow at my lame topic transition, "um, so I have something to tell you, and I'd like to do it over dinner and wine tonight."

"Why can't you tell me now?"

"Because we're at work."

"And yet you mentioned wanting to talk, which means you're nervous and actually need to have the discussion sooner, rather than later."

I chuckle. "Yes, okay. Let's go to the office. But you stay five feet away at all times."

Her innocent look doesn't work on me. Allegra likes to get frisky in the bookstore, and I have zero willpower. My office desk has seen some things, let me tell you.

We keep the mandatory distance and settle into our seats.

Here goes nothing.

"I resigned."

"Resigned what?"

"My position as the store manager. Here at Wood's Writing Emporium."

"Okay. Is there something wrong? Did Clive give you shit about me hanging around? I'll stay away if it's a problem."

"No, nothing like that. Um, well, I've been working towards something, and I'm ready to go for it."

She crosses one leg over the other, and it's a stance I know well. Her boss mode, as I call it.

"And what are you ready to go for, my love?"

Allegra calling me her love, sends shivers down my spine.

"I'm going to be a freelance book editor. In Italy."

Her tongue swipes across her lower lip. "In Italy?"

"Yes. Sicily, to be precise. There's this villa I'd like to live in. What do you think?"

"I think I'm about to break the five-feet rule," she growls, getting up and stalking towards me. I stand to meet her halfway. We kiss and ignite. I'm taking it she's happy with my announcement. Her hands drop to the hem of my skirt, which she then hikes up above my hips. My knickers are pulled to the floor, and I'm pushed back into my office chair.

Allegra drops to her knees. The floor is dusty and I'm instantly worried about her very expensive trousers getting mucky. I'm the only one concerned, though, because Allegra's attention is solely on her prize, which sits between my legs and is aching for her tongue.

She looks up with a grin. "I love you, Bonnie." And then she descends.

Her mouth is extraordinarily good. I'm writhing in place in no time at all. The only thing that could make it better is... Oh, yeah, she's taken down her hair. My hands grab two fistfuls and pull her closer. Her tongue delicately grazes my clit before she sucks me in. The contrasting sensations drive me over the edge and I cry out... Loudly.

Good job I've quit, because this is definitely a sackable offence, and I've absolutely just traumatised anyone in the store. "Oh...wow," I pant.

"That's just the beginning. I'm going to show you over and over again, just how much I love you when we get home."

Loosening my hands from her hair, I drop them to her face and stroke her cheeks. "Does this mean you're okay with moving back to Italy? I know I should have told you."

"If it's what you want, *bella*, I'm happy to go back."

"Not back, Allegra... Home. It's where you belong, and I belong with you."

She helps me to my feet and to redress. "Your dads will *not* be happy."

"They already know. I pre-warned them weeks ago. I just wanted to be sure this is what you'd want. I know you're happy here, but I see it in your eyes, Al. You miss the vineyard and your family. We're not going back to what it was, so my fathers have no say in it. I trust the pact to be upheld, and I trust *you*. Plus, I think Lorenzo will be happy to come too. He needs a hobby that isn't chatting up my customers."

Allegra laughs. "He's a smooth talker, but it's all for fun. He's still devoted to Maria. He always will be. But yes, I agree he needs something to occupy him. Running the sales at the vineyard would make him happy."

"Will you be happy? If we go back? Mia, Rosa, and Toni will be over the moon to have you home."

She pulls me in. Our lips are an inch apart as those striking eyes bore into me. "Where you are, is where I'm happy. But there is one thing that might make it all the sweeter."

"And what's that?"

"Marry me."

I pull back in shock. Then bite my lip. "Hmm, I said I'd never marry the mob queen."

She smiles. "I'm only Donna Malgeri in the bedroom, baby...at your request."

I blush because she isn't wrong. "I suppose I *did* become your sex slave. Might as well go the whole hog, huh?"

"Is that a yes?"

"It's a hell yes!" I laugh and kiss her. "Will you…"

"I'll dress the part for you tonight, Ms Moorside. Prepare to be seduced."

"*Mob's Seduction*," I titter. "Maybe it's not such a bad title after all."

Allegra bites my nose. "I wouldn't go that far."

Afterword

Thank you for reading Mob's Seduction.
Please spare a few more minutes of your time by heading
over to Amazon and Goodreads to leave a review.

Acknowledgements

A huge thank you to my team and readers, who have been nothing short of fantastic. Your continued support means the world to me.

Other Titles By Alyson Root

A Dance Towards Forever
Diving Into Her
Always Emilie
Broken Parts Included
Love & Other Wild Things
Finding Molly Parsons
Keeping Carmen Ruiz
The Wisdom of Bug
Sleigh Bells Ring
Risking Immortality
Waiting for Eternity
Fighting for Infinity

www.alysonroot.com

About the author

Alyson was born and raised in the heart of England. She moved to Paris in 2015 when she met her wife. Together they moved to the west of France, where they now live with their two dogs. Alyson spends her time reading sapphic fiction books, writing and Scuba Diving.

Alyson discovered her love of writing in her mid-thirties. Her debut book, *A Dance Towards Forever,* was inspired by her wife and their very own love story. Alyson wrote *Diving Into Her* and award-winning *Always Emilie,* which added with her first book, created The French Connection series.

www.alysonroot.com

a.rootauthor@alysonroot.com

HUMAN
AUTHORED™
THE Authors Guild®

4003837